Charlie and the Colourful Clouds

Freya Jobe

Published by Freya Jobe, 2024.

This is a work of fiction. Similarities to real people, places, or events are entirely coincidental.

CHARLIE AND THE COLOURFUL CLOUDS

First edition. November 5, 2024.

Copyright © 2024 Freya Jobe.

ISBN: 979-8227041470

Written by Freya Jobe.

Charlie and the Colorful Clouds

Every morning, Charlie would race to the window, eyes wide with wonder, to gaze at the clouds drifting lazily across the sky. He loved how they floated, soft and fluffy, like cotton candy puffs. But no matter how much he watched, they were always the same shades of white and grey.

One sunny afternoon, something magical happened. As Charlie lay on the grass, staring up at the sky, he spotted a cloud that was unlike any he had ever seen before. This cloud wasn't just white – it shimmered with all the colors of the rainbow, swirling and changing as it floated by.

Charlie could hardly believe his eyes! "Is it really a rainbow... or is it a cloud?" he wondered aloud.

Before he knew it, the cloud drifted closer, as if inviting him to follow. And from that day forward, Charlie's life was filled with the most incredible, colorful adventures high above the ground, in a world where clouds could laugh, dance, and share secrets known only to those who dared to dream.

"Charlie and the Colorful Clouds" is the story of one curious child, a sky full of enchanted clouds, and the unforgettable journey that opened his heart to magic, wonder, and the beauty of every color in the sky.

Chapter 1: A Cloudy Surprise

It was a typical Saturday morning, and Charlie had just finished his breakfast. He slipped on his favorite sneakers and ran out to his backyard, hoping for an adventure. His mom always joked that if there was a hidden treasure or a secret map anywhere around, Charlie would be the one to find it.

Charlie took a deep breath, savouring the cool, fresh air. The sky was mostly clear, with a few scattered clouds drifting lazily overhead. He lay down on the soft grass, folded his arms behind his head, and gazed up, watching the clouds slowly inch across the sky. He loved spotting shapes in the clouds—fluffy animals, swirling castles, and sometimes even faces. He imagined each cloud had its own story, but today, they all seemed ordinary, plain as day.

Just as he was about to close his eyes, something caught his attention. Out of the corner of his eye, Charlie spotted a strange cloud floating just above the tallest tree in his backyard. He blinked, rubbed his eyes, and looked again. It was still there, hanging low in the sky, as if it were waiting for him.

This wasn't like any other cloud he had seen. It looked... different. There was something about it that drew him in, something he couldn't quite explain. It wasn't the shape or the size—it was just different. Charlie couldn't shake the feeling that it was there for a reason, though he didn't know why.

Charlie pushed himself up onto his elbows, staring at the cloud with a curious tilt of his head. The other clouds floated by like normal, drifting wherever the wind took them. But this one seemed to linger, as though it was anchored right above his yard. Almost as if it had chosen to be there.

"What are you doing there, little cloud?" Charlie murmured under his breath. He felt a bit silly talking to it, but somehow, it felt right.

Charlie looked around, wondering if anyone else was seeing this. The neighbours' houses were quiet, and even his own house seemed still, his parents busy inside. It was just him, the wide-open sky, and that strange cloud above.

Feeling a bit braver, Charlie got up and took a step toward the tree. Then another step, and another, craning his neck as he walked. He stopped at the base of the tree, squinting up at the sky. The cloud was still there, exactly where he had first seen it, hovering just out of reach.

Charlie picked up a pebble and tossed it high in the air, trying to see if he could reach it. But of course, the pebble fell back to the ground with a soft plop. He felt silly for even trying, but somehow, he didn't mind. There was something about this cloud that made him feel like he could reach it, as if it were just a little bit closer than all the others.

"Maybe I should climb up," Charlie thought, looking at the sturdy branches of the old tree. He knew his mom wouldn't be thrilled with the idea, but curiosity was already bubbling up inside him. He reached for the lowest branch, testing its strength, and started to climb.

The higher he climbed, the clearer the cloud seemed, though he still couldn't put his finger on why it looked so unique. Charlie wasn't usually afraid of heights, but he felt his heart beating a little faster as he made his way to the top. He was almost within reach of the tallest branch when he stopped, feeling a soft breeze ruffle his hair.

The cloud seemed even closer now, hanging just above him, almost close enough to touch. For a moment, Charlie wondered if he was imagining things. But there it was, as real as the bark under his hands, as real as the sky around him.

Then, suddenly, the cloud moved.

Charlie gasped, nearly losing his grip on the branch. The cloud drifted lower, and for the first time, it seemed to be moving directly toward him. He held his breath, barely daring to blink, watching as it floated closer and closer until it was hovering right in front of him.

Charlie reached out a hand, feeling a tingle of excitement mixed with awe. He wasn't sure if he'd actually be able to touch it, but he couldn't resist trying. His fingers brushed the air just in front of the cloud, and to his surprise, he felt a gentle, cool sensation, like a light mist. He laughed softly, a little nervous, but mostly amazed.

The cloud gave a tiny, almost playful swirl, as if it were responding to him. Charlie blinked, his heart pounding with excitement. Could it... understand him? The thought was wild, impossible. And yet, here it was, swirling in gentle circles, almost as if it were greeting him.

Charlie leaned in closer, his face barely a few inches away. He felt his imagination running wild, thinking of all the stories he could tell his friends about this strange, colorful cloud. But as he stared at it, he realized that none of his stories could capture this moment. There was something magical, something he couldn't put into words.

Then, with a soft whoosh, the cloud drifted away, lifting slightly higher in the air, almost as if it were waving goodbye. Charlie felt a pang of disappointment. He wanted to call out to it, to tell it to stay, but before he could say anything, the cloud started to float away, slowly at first, then a little faster.

Charlie climbed down the tree as quickly as he could, watching as the cloud drifted toward the far end of his yard. He ran after it, his feet pounding against the grass, his eyes fixed on the cloud as it floated just out of reach.

"Wait!" he called, feeling a strange sense of urgency. "Come back!"

But the cloud only drifted higher, floating gently into the distance. Charlie stood there, watching until it was nothing but a faint speck in the sky. He felt a mixture of wonder and sadness, as if he had just let go of something precious.

He stood there for a while, staring at the spot where the cloud had disappeared. It was a feeling he couldn't describe, a strange mixture of joy and longing. He knew he had witnessed something extraordinary, something that would stay with him forever. And though the cloud was gone, he felt certain that this was only the beginning of something magical.

As he turned to go back inside, Charlie took one last look at the sky, a small smile tugging at the corners of his mouth. Somewhere up there, he knew, was a world he had only just glimpsed—a world of colorful clouds, waiting to be discovered.

Chapter 2: The Rainbow Mist

The next morning, Charlie woke up earlier than usual. He couldn't get yesterday's cloud out of his mind. It was unlike anything he had ever seen, and he felt an odd pull, a tug in his chest that seemed to say, Come back outside. So, without even stopping for breakfast, he threw on his jacket, hurried out the door, and dashed into the backyard.

The morning was quiet, the world still waking up. Charlie glanced up at the sky, wondering if he would see another strange cloud, but at first, there was nothing but ordinary wisps of white. His shoulders slumped a bit in disappointment. Maybe it had been a one-time thing, just a strange cloud passing by.

But then, out of nowhere, he saw it again.

There, floating just above the tallest tree, was a cloud—the cloud. It looked exactly like the one he had seen yesterday, only this time it felt closer, as if it had drifted down just for him. Charlie's eyes went wide with excitement. He took a step forward, hardly daring to breathe. He could see it shimmering faintly, as if bathed in an invisible light.

He walked slowly toward it, his footsteps soft on the grass. The closer he got, the clearer the cloud became, until he could see tiny specks of color flickering across its surface. First a glint of red, then a flash of blue, followed by greens, purples, and yellows—every color he could imagine, swirling and dancing together like they were alive.

Charlie's breath caught in his throat. It was a rainbow, but not just any rainbow. This one seemed to be made entirely of mist, each color shifting and changing, blending together in a soft, magical haze.

"Whoa..." he whispered, almost afraid that speaking too loudly would scare it away.

The cloud drifted lower, close enough that Charlie could see each swirl of color weaving in and out, twisting like ribbons in the air. He lifted his hand tentatively, reaching out toward the mist. For a moment, he hesitated, not sure what would happen. But his curiosity got the better of him, and he extended his fingers into the cool, colorful vapor.

To his surprise, it felt soft and gentle, like a morning fog. But it was more than that—there was a tingly feeling too, like the way it feels when you touch a butterfly's wings or run your fingers through sand. The colors seemed to move around his hand, swirling around his fingers in gentle waves. It was as if the mist itself was alive, playfully wrapping itself around him, inviting him to explore.

Charlie grinned, his heart thumping with excitement. He had never felt anything like this before. The mist seemed to shimmer with a soft hum, a faint sound that he could barely hear, as though it were singing in a language he didn't quite understand.

As he watched, the colors shifted, and he thought he could make out shapes in the mist. Maybe he was imagining it, but there seemed to be faint outlines—something like fish, swirling and darting around his hand. He could see the silvery flicker of scales, a flash of a fin, then the mist would shift, and it would be gone, only to be replaced by something else. Now he saw what looked like birds, their feathers brilliant shades of blue and green, flying in and out of the mist like tiny spectres.

Charlie couldn't believe his eyes. He felt like he had discovered a secret world, hidden right there in his own backyard.

"Are you... showing me these?" he asked quietly, feeling a little silly for talking to a cloud. But he couldn't shake the feeling that the mist was somehow responding to him, like it knew he was there. The shapes danced a little faster, and the colors grew even brighter, as if to say, Yes!

Charlie laughed, delighted. It was as if the cloud understood him, like it had been waiting all along to reveal this hidden magic. He took a step closer, his face now only inches away from the mist, and inhaled deeply. It smelled faintly sweet, like fresh flowers after the rain, mixed with something he couldn't quite place, something almost electric.

The mist seemed to swirl even more, and suddenly, Charlie's face was awash with colors. Reds and blues, yellows and greens—it felt like he was standing in the middle of a rainbow. The colors wrapped around him, gentle and warm, and he felt an overwhelming sense of joy, like he was part of something bigger, something magical.

Then, he felt something tickle his cheek—a soft, feathery sensation, as if a tiny piece of the mist had brushed against him. He giggled, reaching up to touch his face, but the mist danced away, swirling and shifting just out of reach.

It felt playful, almost like it was teasing him. Charlie took a step forward, reaching out both hands, and the mist responded, twisting and twirling around his fingers. The colors seemed to pulse with a gentle rhythm, like the beat of a drum, and Charlie found himself swaying along, feeling as though he were dancing with the mist.

For a moment, he closed his eyes, letting the colors wash over him. He felt weightless, like he was floating, carried along by the rhythm of the rainbow mist. In that moment, he felt completely connected to the cloud, as if it were sharing a secret with him, something that only he could understand.

When he opened his eyes, the mist had drifted back a bit, giving him space. He took a deep breath, his heart pounding with excitement. The cloud hovered just in front of him, still shimmering with every color, and he felt a strange sense of gratitude. It was as if the mist had given him a gift, a glimpse into a world he had never known.

Charlie looked up at the cloud, his eyes shining with wonder. He didn't know why it had come, or what it meant, but he knew one thing for certain: this was only the beginning. The cloud hadn't just come to visit—it had come to invite him on an adventure, a journey beyond anything he could have ever imagined.

With one last swirl of color, the mist slowly began to drift upward, rising higher and higher into the sky. Charlie watched, feeling a bittersweet pang as it floated away. He wanted to chase after it, to keep it close, but he knew somehow that it needed to go, that this was only the first of many surprises.

As he watched the cloud disappear into the distance, Charlie felt a warmth in his chest, a quiet certainty. Whatever the mist had shown him, it wasn't over. This was just the beginning of something magical, something that would change everything.

And as he turned back toward the house, Charlie couldn't help but smile, knowing that the rainbow mist would always be there, waiting for him in the sky.

Chapter 3: Meeting Nimbus

The next day, Charlie was back in the backyard, waiting eagerly for the cloud to reappear. His mind was buzzing with questions about the rainbow mist and the shapes he had seen within it. He couldn't shake the feeling that something extraordinary was about to happen, and his heart leaped every time he looked up at the sky.

Just as he was starting to wonder if he'd imagined it all, he saw it—a shimmer on the horizon, a tiny, bright cloud heading his way. It seemed to move with purpose, floating steadily closer, and Charlie could see a soft glow around its edges, like it was bathed in sunlight. His pulse quickened as he watched it approach.

As the cloud got closer, Charlie noticed something odd. This wasn't just a cloud—it was a creature! It had a small, puffy body, plump and soft like a marshmallow, with two bright, twinkling eyes set right in the middle of its fluffy face. Little swirls of vapor floated around it, giving it the look of a friendly, wispy ball of cotton.

Charlie could hardly believe his eyes. He blinked a few times, wondering if he was dreaming, but the cloud creature was still there, drifting down toward him. It hovered at his eye level, close enough that he could see the spark of intelligence and kindness in its bright eyes.

The creature gave a small swirl, almost as if it were nodding a greeting. Charlie's jaw dropped in amazement, and he felt a grin spreading across his face.

"H-hello?" he stammered, feeling a bit silly for talking to a cloud. But then, to his utter surprise, the cloud creature tilted its head and spoke back, in a soft, breezy voice that seemed to drift on the air.

"Hello, Charlie!" it said cheerfully. "I've been waiting for you."

Charlie's eyes widened. "You... you know my name?"

The creature laughed, a sound like the gentle rustle of leaves. "Of course! We clouds know all sorts of things. My name is Nimbus, and I've come to show you our world."

Charlie's heart raced with excitement. "You... you're a cloud? Like, an actual cloud?"

Nimbus gave a playful swirl, a little puff of vapor swirling out from its head like a tiny halo. "Not just any cloud! I'm a special kind of cloud. A cloud guide, you might say. I show people like you the wonders of the sky."

Charlie could barely contain his excitement. "Does that mean... I get to see more of those colorful clouds? And the rainbow mist?"

Nimbus's eyes twinkled. "Oh, you'll see much more than that, my friend! The sky is full of surprises. There's a whole world up there, one that only a few are lucky enough to explore."

Charlie felt his heart swell with wonder. "But... why me?"

Nimbus floated closer, its misty form shimmering in the sunlight. "Because, Charlie, you saw the cloud when others didn't. You looked up, and you believed. That's all it takes to enter the world of clouds. You see, most people look at clouds and think they're just puffs of water in the sky. But you... you saw the magic. And that makes you one of us."

Charlie felt a thrill run through him. He wanted to ask a hundred questions, but all he could manage was, "So... where do we start?"

Nimbus laughed, swirling in the air like a tiny cyclone. "Come on, follow me! I'll show you the first step."

Charlie watched in amazement as Nimbus floated up, a bit higher than the tallest tree. He reached out, hesitating for a moment, but then Nimbus extended a misty arm, inviting him forward. Before he could think too much, Charlie found himself reaching out as well.

To his surprise, he felt himself grow lighter, almost as if his feet had left the ground. A soft, tingling sensation spread through his body, and he realized he was lifting into the air, rising slowly to meet Nimbus. He gasped in amazement, looking down to see his backyard shrinking below him. It was as if he had been wrapped in a soft cocoon of mist, a gentle breeze lifting him higher and higher.

Nimbus beamed at him. "Ready for a skyward adventure, Charlie?"

Charlie nodded, his eyes wide with wonder. "I... I think so!"

With a wink, Nimbus led the way, floating higher, and Charlie followed, feeling as though he were part of a dream. The clouds around him began to shimmer with new colors, soft pastels and glimmers of gold. Each one seemed to have a personality of its own, drifting in gentle, graceful patterns. He could see some clouds twirling together in what looked like a dance, while others shifted into shapes that he could just barely recognize—an animal here, a castle there, all made of vapor and light.

As they drifted higher, Nimbus started pointing things out, explaining in his soft, breezy voice.

"Over there," he said, gesturing to a big, fluffy cloud, "is Fluffy the Cloud. He's the softest cloud around! And over here," Nimbus gestured toward a tall, wispy cloud that stretched into the sky, "that's Cirro, a proud cirrus cloud who watches over the whole sky."

Charlie laughed, taking it all in. He could hardly believe he was actually meeting clouds with names and personalities. "They're... alive?" he asked, still feeling amazed.

Nimbus gave a gentle nod. "In their own way, yes. Each cloud has its own spirit, its own way of being. Some are playful, like Fluffy, and some are a bit serious, like Cirro. And then there are the colorful clouds, the ones you've already seen."

"Where do those come from?" Charlie asked, feeling a surge of curiosity.

Nimbus smiled, his eyes sparkling. "Those are the magic clouds, Charlie. They carry the colors of the rainbow, the whispers of dreams, and the wishes of everyone who looks up at the sky. Only those with open hearts can see them, and only those who truly believe can touch them."

Charlie felt a warmth in his chest as he listened. He had always felt there was something special about the sky, something just beyond what most people noticed. And now, he was seeing it with his own eyes.

Nimbus drifted a bit closer, his voice softening. "You, Charlie, have been chosen to explore the secrets of the clouds. There's so much to see and learn. But remember, this world is delicate. It's a place of wonder, meant to be cherished and protected."

Charlie nodded, his eyes bright with excitement. "I promise, Nimbus. I'll protect it."

Nimbus gave a satisfied nod. "Good. Then, our journey begins."

The two of them floated higher, soaring through the sky as the clouds around them shimmered and danced. Charlie felt a joy he had never known before, a sense of belonging to something bigger, something magical.

As they glided together through the sea of mist and color, Charlie knew that he had found a friend in Nimbus, and a new world in the sky—a world filled with colorful clouds, hidden secrets, and endless adventures.

Chapter 4: The Secret of the Colorful Clouds

Charlie soared through the sky with Nimbus by his side, marveling at the colors swirling around them. The clouds here weren't like the plain white puffs he was used to seeing—they were alive with colors, shifting hues that seemed to pulse and blend, creating patterns that changed with every breeze.

They floated through a soft, glowing mist, with clouds of lavender, turquoise, and rose pink drifting past. Charlie could hardly believe his eyes. The colors seemed to respond to his excitement, brightening and swirling even faster as he and Nimbus glided through them.

At last, Nimbus slowed, hovering near a particularly vibrant cloud that shimmered with flashes of green and gold. He turned to Charlie, his eyes twinkling with warmth and a hint of mystery.

"Charlie," Nimbus began, his voice soft yet filled with wonder, "there's something special about these clouds. They aren't just made of water and air like the others. These clouds hold something much more precious—something invisible to most people."

Charlie leaned in, his curiosity sparked. "What do you mean, Nimbus? What makes them so... colorful?"

Nimbus drifted a little closer, his voice dropping to a whisper. "These clouds, Charlie, change colors based on feelings and imagination."

Charlie's eyes went wide with surprise. "Feelings? Imagination?" he repeated, trying to wrap his mind around the idea.

Nimbus nodded, his expression serious yet kind. "Yes. You see, each of these clouds is a reflection of the thoughts and emotions around it. When someone feels happy, excited, or full of wonder, the cloud might turn bright and warm. But when there's sadness, fear, or worry, the colors fade or darken. They're a mirror of the heart."

Charlie stared in awe at the clouds around him, which seemed to be dancing with bright blues and cheerful yellows. "So... right now, these clouds are... happy?"

Nimbus smiled, a soft laugh escaping him. "Yes, Charlie. They're happy because you're here, and your heart is filled with wonder. These clouds respond to the world, and they love to be near those who believe in magic."

Charlie's heart swelled with joy. He watched as the colors around them brightened, as if the clouds were indeed mirroring his excitement. He reached out, and a streak of soft lavender wrapped around his hand, warm and welcoming.

"Do the colors change a lot?" he asked, thinking of all the emotions he'd felt just since meeting Nimbus.

"Oh, yes," Nimbus replied, nodding. "These clouds are very sensitive. They shift from one color to another whenever the world around them changes. If you think of something you love or feel very deeply about, you might even see a new color appear."

Charlie's mind raced. He closed his eyes, thinking of something that made him feel pure happiness—an image of his family laughing together at a picnic, the sun shining down on them, everyone smiling. When he opened his eyes, he gasped. The cloud in front of him had turned a warm, glowing peach color, with streaks of gold running through it like threads of sunlight.

Nimbus beamed. "See, Charlie? You just shared a piece of your heart with the clouds."

Charlie was amazed. "That's incredible! So... does that mean the clouds are like friends? Do they understand us?"

Nimbus nodded. "In their own way, yes. They feel what you feel and respond with their colors. It's why they're so special—they're filled with kindness and empathy. They carry the emotions of everyone who looks up at them, even if they don't realize it."

Charlie looked around at the sky, wondering if the clouds held the feelings of everyone in his town. He could imagine each cloud carrying a piece of someone's happiness, someone's hope. It made the sky feel alive, filled with connections he had never noticed before.

He watched as one cloud turned a soft green, peaceful and gentle. "What about when someone feels calm or content?" he asked. "Does the cloud change for that too?"

Nimbus chuckled softly. "Absolutely. Calm feelings bring out softer colors, like greens and blues. And when people feel excited or full of laughter, the clouds become vibrant, like the colors of a rainbow. Each feeling has its own shade, its own way of expressing itself."

Charlie couldn't stop smiling. He felt a newfound respect for the clouds, realizing they were more than just parts of the weather. They were like friends, silent yet always there, carrying bits of everyone's heart.

Then a thought struck him. "What happens if someone feels sad or scared? Do the clouds stay colorful?"

Nimbus's expression softened, and he nodded slowly. "No, not always. When people feel sad or lonely, the clouds lose their colors. They become pale, sometimes even grey. But even then, they hold on to the hope that someone will look up and see them, that someone's happiness will bring the color back."

Charlie felt a pang of sympathy. He had always thought of grey clouds as just part of the sky, but now they seemed so much more. "That's... kind of sad," he whispered. "But also beautiful."

Nimbus nodded in agreement. "The clouds are resilient, Charlie. They always find their colors again. Sometimes, all it takes is a bit of laughter, a burst of imagination, or a child looking up with wonder in their eyes."

Charlie smiled. He knew he would never look at a grey cloud the same way again. He felt a deep respect for these colorful clouds, these beautiful mirrors of the world's feelings.

"Do you think... I could make a cloud change color again?" he asked, looking at Nimbus.

Nimbus gave an encouraging nod. "Why don't you try? Think of something that fills you with joy, with excitement. Imagine it as clearly as you can."

Charlie closed his eyes, focusing his thoughts. He imagined a summer evening, playing with his friends, laughing so hard his sides hurt, the warm breeze rustling through the trees. He let the memory fill him with joy, feeling it bubble up like laughter inside him.

When he opened his eyes, the cloud in front of him had turned a brilliant shade of pink, bright and full of energy, like the color of a setting sun. It pulsed softly, as if laughing along with him.

Charlie laughed, delighted by the sight. "I did it! I really did it!"

Nimbus grinned, pride shining in his eyes. "See, Charlie? You're already a natural. The clouds respond to you because you believe, because your heart is open to their magic."

Charlie felt a sense of connection and wonder, a feeling that he belonged to this world of colorful clouds. He realized that he could come back to these clouds anytime, that they would always be there to share his feelings, his dreams.

As they floated back down toward his yard, Charlie looked over at Nimbus. "Thank you," he said softly. "Thank you for showing me this world."

Nimbus gave him a gentle nod. "It's my pleasure, Charlie. You have a special heart—a heart that sees the world in color. And now, the clouds will always be there for you, carrying pieces of your happiness, your imagination, and even your dreams."

As they touched back down in the grass, Charlie knew his life had changed forever. He looked up at the sky with new eyes, filled with appreciation and love for the clouds that mirrored his feelings and those of everyone who looked up to them. And as he waved goodbye to Nimbus, he knew that he would always have friends in the sky—colorful, magical clouds that held secrets, feelings, and endless adventures.

Chapter 5: Painting with the Wind

The following day, Charlie was back outside bright and early, hoping for another chance to see Nimbus and the colorful clouds. The morning sky was a soft shade of blue, dotted with a few fluffy white clouds drifting lazily by. Just as Charlie was beginning to wonder if Nimbus would appear, he heard a familiar breezy voice call out.

"Good morning, Charlie!"

Charlie turned and grinned as Nimbus floated down to meet him, his soft, misty form swirling with excitement. "Good morning, Nimbus! I was hoping you'd come back!"

Nimbus gave a little spin, sending a spiral of mist into the air. "Of course, Charlie! We have a lot more to explore in the world of clouds. Today, I thought we might try something fun. Have you ever wanted to paint a picture in the sky?"

Charlie's eyes went wide. "Paint... in the sky?" He could hardly believe what he was hearing. "How would I even do that?"

Nimbus chuckled, drifting a bit closer. "Well, it's a special trick that only a few know about. You see, with the right kind of focus—and a little help from me—you can create pictures in the sky using the trails of colorful clouds. It's a bit like drawing, but you're using the wind and the mist to shape your art."

Charlie could hardly contain his excitement. He had always loved drawing, but he never imagined he could create pictures up in the sky itself! "How does it work?" he asked eagerly.

Nimbus's eyes sparkled. "All you need is a little imagination and the wind to help you. I'll show you how."

He floated up, higher than the trees, and Charlie followed, feeling lighter and more confident with each step. Nimbus created a gentle breeze that swirled around them, making Charlie feel like he was part of the sky itself.

"Close your eyes, Charlie," Nimbus instructed. "Think of something you'd like to paint. Picture it clearly in your mind."

Charlie closed his eyes, letting his thoughts wander. He thought of something simple but special to him: a big, friendly heart with bright colors, the kind he would draw on cards for his family. He focused on the shape, imagining it bright and cheerful in the sky.

"Got it?" Nimbus asked, his voice like a soft breeze.

Charlie nodded. "I think so."

"Good! Now open your eyes and follow my lead."

Charlie opened his eyes and watched as Nimbus began to float slowly in a large circle, leaving behind a thin, shimmering trail of cloud in his wake. The trail was a soft, rosy pink, and it drifted in the air like a ribbon. Charlie realized that Nimbus was showing him how to "draw" by guiding the cloud with his movements.

Charlie took a deep breath, feeling his heart beat with excitement. He moved his hand, mirroring Nimbus's path, and to his amazement, a soft pink cloud trail followed him, lingering in the air. He laughed in delight, watching as the cloud trailed his movements, like a paintbrush in the sky.

"Now, let's make the heart shape you were thinking of," Nimbus encouraged him.

Charlie focused, tracing the shape of a heart in the air. The cloud trail followed him perfectly, creating a large, friendly heart right there in the sky. He watched as it floated gently, the pink mist shimmering in the morning sunlight. He felt a surge of pride—he had painted a heart in the sky!

Nimbus gave an approving nod. "You're a natural, Charlie! The clouds can sense your intention. All it takes is a clear picture in your mind, and they'll follow your movements."

Charlie beamed, feeling a warm glow of happiness. "Can we try more shapes?" he asked eagerly.

"Of course!" Nimbus replied. "Let's make something colorful this time. Imagine a rainbow of colors, like the ones you saw in the rainbow mist."

Charlie thought for a moment and then pictured a butterfly, its wings spread wide, filled with beautiful colors. He closed his eyes, imagining each detail, and when he opened them, he began to move his hands in gentle arcs, like he was guiding invisible wings.

As he painted, streams of mist in different colors followed his hand, creating a pair of large, graceful wings. The right wing glowed with shades of orange and yellow, while the left wing was tinted with blues and purples. Each color blended softly into the next, like a watercolour painting.

Nimbus watched in delight, encouraging him with each stroke. "You're creating a masterpiece, Charlie! The clouds love colors and shapes, especially when they're made with joy."

Charlie stepped back to admire his creation—a shimmering butterfly floating in the sky, its wings softly glowing with color. It was even better than he'd imagined, a beautiful display of colors that seemed to dance in the breeze.

Then, to Charlie's astonishment, the butterfly began to move! The wings flapped slowly, as if it had come to life, gliding through the sky with gentle, graceful movements.

"Whoa! It's flying!" Charlie gasped, eyes wide with wonder.

Nimbus gave a playful swirl. "Clouds are magical, remember? When you pour your heart into a picture, sometimes it takes on a life of its own."

Charlie watched, mesmerized, as the cloud butterfly drifted across the sky, leaving a faint trail of color in its wake. He couldn't believe he had made something so magical, something that felt alive and full of spirit.

Nimbus drifted closer. "You're doing wonderfully, Charlie. The sky is your canvas, and the wind is your brush. As long as you can imagine it, you can paint it here."

Charlie spent the next few minutes practicing, creating shapes and figures he loved—a sun with long, golden rays, a field of flowers made from swirling purple and yellow clouds, and even a small rainbow that arched across the sky. Each creation floated in the air, shimmering with color and life, adding beauty to the world above.

As he worked, Nimbus taught him how to use the wind to guide the clouds. "The wind is gentle but powerful," Nimbus explained. "If you listen closely, you'll feel its direction. Just follow its flow, and your pictures will come to life."

Charlie focused, feeling the wind's soft tug as he moved. With Nimbus's help, he learned to let the breeze carry his cloud trails, watching as his pictures gently floated across the sky, like drawings on a grand, open canvas.

After a while, Charlie sat back, taking a deep breath. His heart felt light, his spirit filled with joy and a sense of wonder. He looked up at the sky, now dotted with his colorful creations, and he knew he would never forget this feeling.

"Thank you, Nimbus," he said softly. "This is the most amazing thing I've ever done."

Nimbus's eyes shone with pride. "You did this, Charlie. You brought your imagination to life, and the clouds were happy to help. The sky is always here for you, whenever you want to paint again."

Charlie looked out over his skyward creations, feeling a deep sense of gratitude. He knew he had discovered something precious, something he could always return to.

As the morning sun climbed higher, he watched his colorful cloud paintings drift and fade, blending back into the sky. But Charlie knew that these creations, these memories, would stay with him forever, floating in his heart like colorful clouds on the breeze.

Chapter 6: The Cloud Castle

After several days of exploring the sky with Nimbus, Charlie felt like he had seen more magic than he could have ever dreamed of. He'd painted pictures in the sky, learned the secrets of colorful clouds, and even made friends with clouds who had their own personalities. But today, Nimbus had a glimmer in his eye, as if he had saved something truly special for last.

"Charlie," Nimbus began, his misty voice carrying a hint of mystery, "have you ever wondered if there's something... hidden up here? A place only the clouds know about?"

Charlie's heart skipped a beat. He loved secrets and hidden places. "A hidden place in the sky?" he echoed, wide-eyed. "Is there really something like that?"

Nimbus gave a small, playful swirl. "Indeed there is. And today, if you're ready, I think it's time I showed you."

Charlie's pulse quickened with excitement. "I'm ready!"

With a nod, Nimbus began to float higher, guiding Charlie through a path of soft clouds that looked almost like a winding road in the sky. Charlie followed, feeling a sense of awe as he looked around. The air grew lighter, and the colors around him softened into gentle pastels, like the beginning of a sunset.

After a few minutes of drifting through the mist, Charlie began to notice something strange—a faint shimmer in the distance. He squinted, trying to make out the shape. At first, it looked like a mirage, like a sparkle on the horizon. But as they got closer, Charlie's breath caught in his throat.

It was a castle, made entirely of clouds.

The castle was enormous, with tall towers that seemed to touch the very top of the sky, their tips shimmering with soft, golden light. The walls were built from thick, billowing clouds, giving the structure a dreamlike appearance, as though it might vanish at any moment. Tiny cloud wisps curled around it like vines, and its windows glowed faintly, as if they held hidden lights inside.

Nimbus floated to Charlie's side, his eyes filled with pride and excitement. "Welcome to the Cloud Castle," he said softly. "A hidden sanctuary in the sky, known only to a few."

Charlie's jaw dropped as he stared up at the majestic structure. "It's... it's incredible," he whispered, feeling as though he were standing in a dream.

Nimbus led him closer, and as they reached the entrance—a grand archway framed by swirling clouds—Charlie felt a tingling sensation, as if he were stepping into a place filled with ancient magic. Inside, everything glowed with a faint sparkle, and the air was filled with a soft, soothing hum, like distant music carried on the wind.

The floor of the castle was made of mist, soft yet solid under his feet, and each step sent tiny puffs of sparkling cloud dust into the air. Sunlight filtered through the castle walls, casting a gentle, golden glow that made everything feel warm and welcoming.

Charlie looked around, taking in the sights. There were spiralling staircases made from clouds, archways that led to hidden rooms, and grand windows that opened to breathtaking views of the endless sky. It was like something out of a fairy tale, a castle in the clouds that seemed to stretch on forever.

"This place is amazing, Nimbus!" he said, spinning around in wonder. "Who made it? How did it get here?"

Nimbus smiled, drifting alongside him. "No one knows exactly how it came to be. Some say the castle formed when the very first dreams drifted up into the sky. Others believe it was built by the oldest, wisest clouds, to hold the secrets of the world. But one thing is certain—it's a place filled with magic, a place where dreams and wishes come to rest."

As they moved through the castle, Nimbus showed Charlie hidden rooms and passageways. One room held shelves made of cloud layers, filled with glimmering objects that looked like tiny stars. Another room was like a gallery, with walls that displayed ever-changing pictures, images made entirely of coloured mist. Each picture told a different story—a child laughing, a family hugging, a forest filled with sunlight—all moving like scenes in a magical movie.

"What are these?" Charlie asked, watching in awe as the images shifted before his eyes.

"These are memories," Nimbus explained gently. "Every cloud carries memories, pieces of the world it's drifted over. And here, in the castle, those memories come to life, like living pictures."

Charlie stared at the images, feeling a deep sense of wonder. It was as if the castle held fragments of life from everywhere—bits of happiness, hope, and love, all preserved in the walls of mist.

They continued exploring, and soon Nimbus led him to a large, open room at the very top of the tallest tower. The walls were open to the sky, and a gentle breeze drifted through, carrying the scent of fresh rain. In the center of the room was a throne, made of soft, fluffy clouds and decorated with sparkling droplets of mist.

Nimbus gestured toward it, his eyes twinkling. "Go ahead, Charlie. Try it out."

Charlie hesitated, then climbed onto the throne, feeling the soft mist mold perfectly around him, as if it had been waiting for him all along. He felt a strange energy, a sense of connection to everything around him, as though he were part of the sky itself.

"Charlie," Nimbus said softly, floating next to him, "the Cloud Castle is a place of wonder, a place where the sky's magic is at its strongest. Only those who truly believe can see it, and only those with open hearts can enter."

Charlie looked around, feeling a warmth fill him. "I feel like I'm part of it," he murmured. "Like... like this place knows me."

Nimbus gave a small nod. "The castle recognizes those who love the clouds and see the magic in them. It's been here for as long as the sky itself, waiting for people like you."

Charlie's heart swelled with happiness. He had always loved the sky, always felt a sense of wonder whenever he looked up. And now, here he was, sitting on a throne in a castle made of clouds, surrounded by colors and memories, by pieces of the world he had only dreamed of.

After a few peaceful moments, Nimbus floated over, a gentle smile on his face. "Are you ready to see something even more special?"

Charlie's eyes sparkled with excitement. "There's more?"

Nimbus nodded, then gestured toward one of the archways. Charlie followed him to the edge of the room, where a wide balcony overlooked the entire sky. From this height, Charlie could see the whole world stretched out below him, tiny and shimmering, as if he were looking down from a great mountaintop.

Nimbus pointed to a faint glimmer in the distance. "Out there," he said softly, "is a place only the clouds know about. It's called the Horizon of Dreams. It's where all the wishes and hopes people make float up to, where they rest before they journey back to earth as dreams. The Cloud Castle watches over it, protecting those dreams."

Charlie's heart filled with awe. "The clouds really carry dreams?" he asked in wonder.

"Yes," Nimbus replied. "Dreams, wishes, hopes—they all find their way to the sky, traveling through the clouds. And here, in the castle, we hold them close, making sure they're safe until it's time for them to find someone who needs them."

Charlie looked out at the horizon, feeling a deep sense of peace. He knew he would never forget this place, this castle in the sky filled with dreams and memories. It was a place of magic, of kindness, a hidden sanctuary in the clouds.

As they prepared to leave, Charlie turned to Nimbus, his eyes filled with gratitude. "Thank you for showing me this, Nimbus. It's the most beautiful thing I've ever seen."

Nimbus smiled, his eyes soft. "It's my pleasure, Charlie. The Cloud Castle will always be here, waiting for you whenever you want to return."

Charlie took one last look at the castle, taking in every detail, every sparkle of mist and shimmer of light. He knew that even though he was leaving, a part of him would always be here, in this hidden castle of clouds, where dreams and memories were kept safe.

And as he drifted back down to earth with Nimbus, Charlie knew that he would carry the magic of the Cloud Castle in his heart forever, a secret place he could always return to whenever he looked up at the sky.

Chapter 7: The Mischievous Storm Cloud

Charlie was floating along with Nimbus, still basking in the memory of the Cloud Castle, when he noticed a dark shape creeping into the bright, cheerful sky. At first, he thought it was just a shadow, maybe from a passing cloud, but as he looked closer, he realized it was something else entirely.

A thick, grey cloud was drifting toward them, darker and more ominous than any cloud he'd seen up close before. This cloud seemed to carry a weight with it, a heavy, rumbling energy that made the hairs on the back of his neck stand up.

Nimbus noticed it too. He let out a soft sigh and said, "Oh dear. It looks like Thunder is coming to visit."

Charlie felt a twinge of nervousness. "Thunder? Who's that?"

Nimbus drifted closer to him, his voice a mixture of caution and warmth. "Thunder is... well, let's just say he's a bit of a troublemaker. He's a storm cloud, and sometimes he gets a little too excited. When he's around, things can get a bit, well... unpredictable."

As if on cue, the dark cloud gave a low, rumbling growl that sounded almost like laughter. Charlie gulped, watching as Thunder drew closer. Unlike the other clouds, which seemed light and joyful, Thunder carried a restless energy. Small flashes of lightning sparked around him, and every so often, he let out a grumbling rumble, like a belly full of thunder.

Thunder floated up beside them, looking at Nimbus with a mischievous glint in his smoky eyes. "Nimbus," he said in a deep, booming voice, "what are you doing with this little human?"

Nimbus offered a polite nod. "Hello, Thunder. This is Charlie. He's our friend, and he's here to learn about the magic of the clouds."

Thunder looked at Charlie with a smirk. "Magic of the clouds, eh?" he scoffed. "Well, I'll show him some real cloud power."

Before Nimbus could say anything, Thunder took a big, deep breath, puffing himself up. Dark, swirling clouds formed around him, and Charlie could feel the air grow heavy. Then, with a loud crack, Thunder let out a bolt of lightning that flashed across the sky, lighting up the clouds in bright white. The rumble that followed made Charlie jump, his heart racing.

"Isn't that better?" Thunder chuckled, clearly amused by the effect his stormy display had on Charlie.

Nimbus sighed, shaking his head. "Thunder, we're just trying to enjoy the day. There's no need for all this noise."

But Thunder wasn't listening. He was having too much fun. He zoomed around, sending little shockwaves and bursts of thunder with every twist and turn, his laughter booming through the sky. Charlie winced as Thunder created a gust of wind that whipped around him, making the clouds swirl in chaotic patterns.

Charlie glanced over at Nimbus, who looked both disappointed and a little worried. Nimbus floated closer to Charlie, whispering, "Sometimes Thunder can be... a bit hard to handle. He loves being the center of attention and tends to get carried away."

Charlie nodded, watching Thunder create little flashes of lightning, followed by loud bursts of thunder. He could see that Thunder was full of energy, but it didn't seem like he was trying to be mean. He was just... well, a little wild.

Charlie took a deep breath, trying to steady his nerves. He wanted to help calm Thunder down, but he wasn't sure how. Then he remembered something his mom always said about dealing with people who seemed a little rough on the outside: Sometimes they just need someone to listen, to help them find their calm.

Gathering his courage, Charlie floated closer to Thunder, who was still laughing and swirling around. "Um... hey, Thunder?" he called out.

Thunder paused mid-rumble, looking at Charlie with curiosity. "Yes, little human?" he said, smirking.

Charlie swallowed, his heart beating a little faster. "I... I saw your lightning. It was really impressive! You're really powerful."

Thunder looked taken aback, as if he wasn't used to compliments. "Well, of course I am! I'm Thunder, after all!" he boomed, puffing up with pride.

Charlie nodded, smiling. "Yeah! I bet you can do all sorts of cool things. But, uh... have you ever tried using your power to make something beautiful?"

Thunder blinked, clearly puzzled. "Beautiful? What do you mean?"

Charlie thought for a moment, then pointed to the horizon, where soft, glowing clouds floated peacefully. "What if you tried making something with your lightning? Like a design in the sky? I think it would look amazing."

Thunder tilted his head, clearly intrigued. "A design? Hmm..." He thought about it, his dark clouds swirling thoughtfully. "I've never tried that before."

Nimbus gave Charlie an encouraging nod. "Go on, Thunder. Show us what you can create. You might surprise yourself."

Thunder looked from Nimbus to Charlie, then let out a thoughtful hum. "Alright, then. Watch this!"

He floated back a bit, closing his eyes and gathering his energy. Charlie watched as Thunder's clouds grew darker, swirling together. Then, with a soft crackle, he released a burst of lightning—not in a random bolt, but in a gentle arc that curved through the sky, creating a zigzagging line that glowed bright and then faded into soft sparkles.

Charlie gasped in delight. "Wow, Thunder! That was amazing!"

Thunder opened one eye, watching Charlie's reaction with interest. "You... you really think so?"

Charlie nodded enthusiastically. "Absolutely! You made a lightning trail that looked like a shooting star!"

Thunder looked down, a small, almost bashful smile forming on his misty face. "I guess I did, didn't I?"

Nimbus floated over, his voice warm with approval. "See, Thunder? You don't always have to be loud to be powerful. Sometimes, a bit of grace goes a long way."

Thunder seemed to think about this, looking at the soft sparkle left behind by his lightning trail. He sighed, his clouds growing a little lighter. "I guess... I guess I don't always have to make a big boom," he admitted, his voice softer than before. "Sometimes it's nice to be appreciated, even when I'm quiet."

Charlie smiled, feeling a warmth in his heart. "I think you're really cool, Thunder. The way you can create lightning and thunder—it's incredible! You have so much strength, but you can use it however you like. It doesn't always have to be loud."

Thunder's eyes softened, and he let out a small, gentle rumble. "Thank you, Charlie. I don't think anyone's ever said that to me before."

Nimbus beamed with pride as Thunder's dark clouds faded, turning a soft shade of grey, with gentle hints of blue and white. He seemed calmer now, more at peace. "Well, Charlie, it seems you've made a new friend," Nimbus said, his voice filled with warmth.

Thunder gave Charlie a nod. "If you ever need a little extra power in the sky, you know who to call." He gave a small, playful zap of lightning, but this time it was gentle, like a friendly wave.

Charlie laughed, feeling a sense of accomplishment. He had helped Thunder see his strength in a new way, one that didn't rely on making loud noises or causing chaos. He knew that Thunder would still be a storm cloud, wild and full of energy, but now he could also be a friend.

As Thunder drifted away, leaving a soft, shimmering trail behind him, Charlie looked over at Nimbus, his heart filled with pride and happiness. "Thanks, Nimbus. I didn't think I could calm him down."

Nimbus placed a gentle misty hand on Charlie's shoulder. "You reminded him of his beauty, Charlie. You showed him that his power could be used in ways he'd never thought of. That's a gift, my friend."

Charlie looked out at the horizon, watching as Thunder floated peacefully away. He knew that he would never forget this day, the day he helped a storm cloud find its calm and turned thunder into beauty.

Chapter 8: The Sky Garden

After their adventure with Thunder, Nimbus floated over to Charlie, a gentle smile on his face. "Charlie," he began, "how would you like to see something truly rare? A place so magical that only a few clouds know about it?"

Charlie's eyes sparkled with curiosity. "More magical than the Cloud Castle?" he asked, hardly able to imagine anything more enchanting.

Nimbus chuckled. "This place is different—full of life, color, and beauty. It's a place where colors bloom like never before. Follow me, and I'll show you."

With that, Nimbus led Charlie higher into the sky. They drifted through gentle wisps of mist, and the air grew softer, filled with a subtle, sweet fragrance. As they moved forward, Charlie noticed the mist growing thicker, swirling with faint shades of pastel colors. Soon, the colors deepened, and Charlie began to see shapes within the mist—soft, petal-like forms in hues of pink, blue, and lavender, glowing gently in the soft light.

When Nimbus finally slowed down, Charlie realized they had arrived at a floating meadow—a garden suspended in the sky. His jaw dropped as he took in the sight.

Spanning as far as he could see, a garden of flowers bloomed right there in the clouds. Each flower was unique, formed from soft puffs of cloud, with petals that glowed in every color imaginable. Some were as small as his thumb, while others towered over him like shimmering trees. The flowers seemed to sway gently in the breeze, their colors shifting and blending, like they were made of rainbows woven into mist.

"Welcome to the Sky Garden," Nimbus said softly, watching Charlie's amazement with a smile. "This is a sacred place where flowers bloom from clouds and colors are alive. Each flower here carries the dreams and hopes of the world below."

Charlie was speechless, his eyes wide with wonder. "It's... beautiful. I've never seen anything like it," he whispered, taking a step forward. He reached out to touch one of the smaller flowers, a delicate bloom with soft, shimmering petals in shades of blue and silver. As his fingers brushed its surface, it felt cool and light, like touching a gentle mist. The flower gave a faint glow in response, as if greeting him.

Nimbus drifted closer, pointing to a cluster of flowers that sparkled with hues of yellow and green. "Each flower here blooms from a special kind of cloud," he explained. "They grow from kindness, hope, joy... emotions that fill the world and drift up here to bloom."

Charlie's heart swelled as he looked around, seeing the garden with new eyes. These flowers weren't just beautiful—they held the emotions of people from everywhere, growing in the sky like precious treasures.

He wandered deeper into the garden, marveling at each flower. Some flowers glowed softly, while others sparkled like tiny stars. He saw blossoms shaped like suns, petals that looked like rainbows, and buds that shimmered with swirling colors he could hardly describe. Every flower seemed to carry a unique feeling, a tiny piece of the world's heart.

"Look at this one!" Charlie called to Nimbus, pointing at a large, fiery red bloom that pulsed gently with light.

Nimbus floated over, nodding with a soft smile. "Ah, that one grew from a wish. A child somewhere on earth wished for courage, and that wish took root here in the garden. The flower blooms as a reminder of their bravery."

Charlie looked at the flower, feeling a rush of pride and admiration for the child who had made that wish. He knew that each flower here was special, each one a reminder of something beautiful in the world below.

Then he noticed something unusual—a small patch of flowers off to the side, with petals that seemed dimmer than the others. The flowers there were a pale grey, their colors faded and soft.

"Why do these flowers look so different?" Charlie asked, walking over to the patch of grey blooms.

Nimbus followed him, his expression thoughtful. "These flowers grew from feelings of sadness or loneliness," he explained gently. "They may not be as bright as the others, but they're just as important. Even in sadness, there's beauty. And these flowers bloom to remind us that no feeling is ever forgotten here."

Charlie reached out to touch one of the grey flowers, feeling a gentle warmth. It was soft and delicate, its color subtle yet comforting. As he touched it, the flower seemed to brighten slightly, a faint hint of color returning to its petals.

Nimbus nodded approvingly. "You see, Charlie, even a little kindness can bring light back to the world. Every touch of care, every moment of love, adds color to the garden."

Charlie looked around, feeling a sense of purpose. He reached out and touched a few more of the grey flowers, watching as each one brightened slightly, their petals glowing softly under his hand. He felt as if he were connecting with each feeling, bringing a bit of hope and kindness to each flower he touched.

As they moved on, Nimbus led Charlie to a part of the garden filled with flowers that seemed to sparkle like stars. Their petals were silver and gold, with tiny sparkles that flickered and danced.

"These are Dream Blooms," Nimbus said in a reverent tone. "They're born from the wishes people make as they drift off to sleep. Dreams of adventures, of friendship, of peace... they all bloom here."

Charlie felt a shiver of excitement as he touched one of the Dream Blooms. It felt cool and soft, and as he looked closer, he thought he could see tiny images dancing within its petals—a child playing with a puppy, a family sharing a meal, a city full of lights. Each dream flickered within the flower, like a tiny story waiting to unfold.

"This place is amazing, Nimbus," Charlie said, his voice filled with awe. "I wish everyone could see it."

Nimbus placed a gentle misty hand on Charlie's shoulder. "They do, in their own way. Every time someone looks up at the clouds and smiles, every time they send a wish into the sky, they're connecting with this place. The Sky Garden may be hidden, but it's always there, quietly blooming for everyone."

Charlie felt a deep sense of peace as he looked around the garden. He knew he was standing in a place of magic, a place where beauty and hope bloomed without end. Each flower was a testament to the power of emotions, the strength of dreams, and the beauty of every feeling.

As they prepared to leave, Charlie turned to Nimbus, his heart full of gratitude. "Thank you for bringing me here, Nimbus. I'll never forget it."

Nimbus nodded, his voice soft. "The Sky Garden will always be here, Charlie, just like the clouds above. Every time you look up at the sky, remember that beauty, hope, and kindness are always blooming, even if you can't see them."

With one last look at the glowing flowers, Charlie took Nimbus's hand, and together, they drifted away from the garden, carrying its magic and warmth in their hearts.

As they floated back toward his backyard, Charlie knew he would always remember the Sky Garden—a place of endless colors, blooming high in the sky, carrying the dreams and wishes of everyone on earth.

Chapter 9: A Rainy Day Challenge

It had been a few days since Charlie's last adventure in the Sky Garden, and he was already itching for more time in the clouds with Nimbus. That morning, however, as he sat at the breakfast table, he overheard his parents talking in worried tones.

"It's been weeks since we've had any rain," his mom was saying, frowning as she looked out the window at the parched lawn. "The plants are struggling, and the garden is barely holding on."

His dad nodded, folding up the newspaper. "The weather report doesn't show any rain coming soon, either. The whole town is in a dry spell."

Charlie listened, his heart sinking as he thought of the plants and flowers in his backyard, of the fields and gardens that needed water. His parents and neighbours had tried everything to keep their gardens alive, but without rain, the ground was dry and cracked.

An idea popped into Charlie's mind, and he felt his pulse quicken with excitement. Maybe I can help! He quickly finished his breakfast, slipped outside, and called up to the sky.

"Nimbus! Nimbus, are you there?" he called, looking up with hope.

After a moment, a familiar wisp of mist appeared, and Nimbus floated down toward him, his eyes twinkling with warmth. "Good morning, Charlie! You called?"

Charlie looked up at his cloud friend, determination in his eyes. "Nimbus, my town really needs rain. There hasn't been any for weeks, and everything is starting to dry out. Do you think... maybe... I could learn how to bring rain to help?"

Nimbus smiled, impressed by Charlie's thoughtfulness. "That's a noble request, Charlie. Controlling rain clouds is one of the most delicate skills a cloud keeper can have. But I believe you're ready for the challenge."

Charlie's face lit up with excitement. "Really? You think I can do it?"

Nimbus nodded, drifting a little higher. "Of course! We'll need to find a few friendly rain clouds willing to help, and I'll show you how to guide them. It's all about balance and focus—too much rain, and we could cause flooding; too little, and it won't make a difference."

Charlie nodded seriously, feeling the weight of the task. He knew it wouldn't be easy, but he was determined to try.

"Come with me," Nimbus said, and he began drifting toward the open sky. Charlie followed, feeling a thrill of excitement as they rose higher. The air grew cooler as they went, and soon, they reached a part of the sky where thick, grey clouds floated in clusters.

Nimbus gestured to a few clouds nearby, each one plump and soft, with tiny droplets of water glistening along their edges. "These are rain clouds, ready to release their water when needed. They just need a little guidance to know where to go and how much to release."

Charlie reached out, feeling the cool mist of the nearest cloud. He could sense its energy, calm yet heavy, as if it were holding onto something precious. "How do I guide them?" he asked, looking up at Nimbus.

Nimbus smiled encouragingly. "Close your eyes, Charlie. Think about your town, your garden, and all the plants that need water. Picture it clearly in your mind. The rain clouds will respond to your thoughts and emotions."

Charlie closed his eyes, focusing on the memory of his backyard, the thirsty flowers and plants he loved. He thought of the town's fields and gardens, picturing how they would brighten up with fresh rain, how the soil would turn rich and damp, how everything would feel alive again.

As he concentrated, he felt a gentle warmth building in his chest, a deep feeling of care and love for the world around him. When he opened his eyes, he saw that the clouds had drifted closer, as if they'd heard his silent call.

"They're listening to you, Charlie," Nimbus said with pride. "Now, let's guide them toward the town."

Charlie extended his hand, as he'd done when painting with cloud trails, and took a deep breath. Moving slowly, he gestured for the clouds to follow him, imagining them gliding toward his town. To his delight, the clouds moved, drifting gently in the direction of his thoughts.

"Great job, Charlie!" Nimbus encouraged. "Now, the tricky part. You need to help them release just the right amount of rain. Too much, and it could overwhelm the plants."

Charlie nodded, feeling the importance of the task. He focused on the clouds, picturing them releasing a gentle, steady rain—just enough to soak the soil without causing any harm.

Taking a deep breath, he closed his eyes again and whispered, "Please, bring just the right amount of rain."

When he opened his eyes, the clouds began to darken, and he heard a soft, distant rumble. Tiny droplets formed on the edges of the clouds, and before long, a gentle rain began to fall. It started as a light drizzle, then grew into a steady, refreshing shower.

Charlie watched in awe as the rain drifted down, soaking the town below. He felt a deep sense of accomplishment, knowing that he had helped bring this life-giving water to the earth.

Nimbus hovered beside him, beaming with pride. "You did it, Charlie! You brought rain just where it was needed."

Charlie looked down, watching as the rain sprinkled over his backyard and the fields beyond. He could see the plants perk up, their leaves glistening as they drank in the water. It was as if the whole town were coming alive, refreshed and renewed.

After a few minutes, Nimbus placed a gentle hand on Charlie's shoulder. "Now, let's ease off the rain. The plants have had a good drink, but too much could wash the soil away."

Charlie nodded, reaching out to the clouds once more. He thought of sunshine, of gentle warmth after the rain, and slowly, the clouds began to lighten. The rain softened to a light drizzle, then stopped altogether, leaving the air fresh and cool.

As the clouds drifted apart, rays of sunlight broke through, casting a warm glow over the landscape. Charlie felt a swell of pride as he looked down at his town, the gardens now bright with droplets of water that sparkled in the sunlight.

Nimbus turned to him, his eyes shining. "You did wonderfully, Charlie. Rain is one of the most precious gifts a cloud can give, and today, you brought it with care and respect."

Charlie grinned, feeling a deep sense of accomplishment. "Thank you, Nimbus. I couldn't have done it without you."

Nimbus gave him a gentle nudge. "The sky is always here for those who care, Charlie. You brought life to your town today. Remember, the power to help is always within you."

As they floated back toward his backyard, Charlie looked down, watching as the gardens, fields, and flowers glistened in the sunlight. He knew that the town would be grateful for the rain, even if they didn't know how it had come.

And as he touched down on the soft, damp grass, Charlie looked up at the sky, a sense of peace and pride filling his heart. He knew that whenever his town needed help, he could always look to the clouds, ready to lend a gentle hand.

Chapter 10: The Dance of the Firefly Clouds

That evening, as the sun dipped below the horizon, Charlie lay on his bed, gazing out the window at the darkening sky. His day of bringing rain to the town had filled him with a sense of pride and wonder, but he felt like there was something more waiting for him up in the clouds tonight. He had seen so much magic in the sky already, but Nimbus had hinted that there were still secrets the night held—secrets that could only be seen in darkness.

Unable to resist the call of the night sky, Charlie slipped quietly out of bed, wrapped himself in his jacket, and crept out into the backyard. The air was cool and calm, filled with the gentle sounds of crickets and the soft rustling of leaves in the breeze. He took a deep breath, savouring the quiet beauty of the evening.

"Charlie," a familiar voice called softly from above.

Charlie looked up to see Nimbus drifting down, his form glowing faintly in the moonlight.

"You came!" Charlie whispered, smiling up at his cloud friend.

Nimbus nodded, his eyes twinkling with excitement. "I wanted to show you something special tonight. There's a part of the sky that only comes alive after the sun goes down—a dance that only the night knows."

Charlie's eyes widened in anticipation. "A dance?"

Nimbus nodded, drifting up a little higher. "Yes. Tonight, the firefly clouds will light up the sky, and if you listen closely, you might just hear their song."

Charlie's heart filled with excitement. He'd never heard of firefly clouds before, and the idea of dancing in the night sky with glowing clouds sounded like the most magical thing he could imagine.

"Come on," Nimbus said, offering Charlie a misty hand. Charlie took it, feeling the cool, comforting touch of his cloud friend as they floated higher into the night sky. They drifted up, above the trees and rooftops, until they reached a place where the stars shone brightly, filling the sky with tiny, twinkling lights.

Just as Charlie was beginning to wonder where the firefly clouds were, he saw a faint glow in the distance. At first, it was just a small flicker, like the light of a single firefly. But then, more lights appeared, one after another, until the entire sky seemed to be filled with tiny, glowing clouds.

Charlie gasped in wonder. The clouds were small and delicate, each one pulsing with a soft, golden light, just like fireflies. They moved gracefully through the sky, floating and swirling together in intricate patterns, their lights twinkling in time with each other.

"These are the firefly clouds," Nimbus explained, his voice filled with reverence. "They only come out at night, lighting up the sky with their gentle glow. They're born from dreams and wishes that people make as they drift off to sleep. Tonight, they're putting on a special dance."

Charlie watched in awe as the firefly clouds drifted and spun, forming beautiful patterns in the air. Some clouds swirled together in small clusters, creating spirals of light, while others moved alone, trailing glowing wisps behind them like comets. The air was filled with a soft, musical hum, a sound so gentle it was almost like a lullaby.

"It's beautiful," Charlie whispered, unable to look away.

Nimbus smiled, his own glow blending with the soft lights around them. "Would you like to join the dance?"

Charlie's eyes sparkled with excitement. "Can I?"

"Of course," Nimbus replied with a nod. "All you need to do is listen to the rhythm of the sky, and let your heart guide you."

Charlie took a deep breath, feeling the cool night air fill his lungs. He closed his eyes, letting the gentle hum of the firefly clouds fill his senses. It was a soft, lilting tune, a melody that seemed to drift through the sky, rising and falling like the waves of the ocean.

As he focused on the sound, he felt himself begin to move, swaying gently in time with the rhythm. He opened his eyes and saw that he was glowing faintly, his body wrapped in a soft, golden light that matched the firefly clouds around him.

Charlie laughed in delight, spinning and twirling through the air, moving in harmony with the glowing clouds. He felt weightless, like he was part of the sky itself, a tiny spark in the vast expanse of stars and moonlight. The firefly clouds danced around him, their lights flickering and pulsing in time with his movements.

Nimbus joined in, drifting beside him, swirling and spinning in graceful arcs. Together, they danced among the firefly clouds, their laughter echoing softly in the night. Charlie felt a sense of joy and freedom like never before, as if he were part of a great, beautiful secret that only the sky knew.

As they danced, Charlie noticed that the firefly clouds seemed to respond to their movements. When he reached out his hand, a cluster of clouds drifted closer, twinkling like tiny stars. He spun in a circle, and the clouds followed, forming a spiral of light around him.

Nimbus floated beside him, his voice soft and full of warmth. "The firefly clouds are drawn to joy and wonder. They dance for those who believe in magic, those who carry light in their hearts."

Charlie felt his heart swell with happiness as he twirled through the sky, his movements light and free. He danced with the firefly clouds, moving in time with the rhythm of the night, each step filling him with a sense of connection to the world around him.

After a while, Nimbus slowed, and the firefly clouds drifted to a gentle stop, their lights softening to a warm glow. Charlie felt a peaceful calm settle over him, and he looked out at the sky, filled with gratitude for this magical moment.

As they floated back down to the ground, Charlie looked up at Nimbus, his eyes filled with wonder. "Thank you for bringing me here, Nimbus. I'll never forget the Dance of the Firefly Clouds."

Nimbus smiled, placing a gentle hand on Charlie's shoulder. "The night sky holds many wonders, Charlie. And tonight, you became part of one of its most beautiful secrets. The firefly clouds will always remember you."

Charlie looked up at the sky, watching as the firefly clouds drifted higher, their lights twinkling softly in the distance. He knew that he had been part of something truly magical, a dance that would stay with him forever, glowing like a memory of starlight in his heart.

As he lay down in the grass, looking up at the dark, star-filled sky, Charlie felt a deep sense of peace. He knew that whenever he looked up at the stars, he would remember the Dance of the Firefly Clouds—a dance of light, dreams, and wonder, waiting for those who dared to believe.

And as he closed his eyes, drifting off to sleep, he knew that somewhere up in the sky, the firefly clouds were still dancing, lighting up the night with their gentle, magical glow.

Chapter 11: Rescuing the Lost Balloon

One breezy afternoon, Charlie was out in his backyard, gazing up at the sky and imagining all the wonders hidden up there. Just as he was wondering what kind of adventure the clouds had in store for him, he spotted a small, bright shape bobbing up and down in the sky.

It was a red balloon, drifting along, but it wasn't floating smoothly like a free spirit. Instead, it was tugging and bouncing as if it were trying to escape from something. Charlie squinted, trying to make sense of the scene, and soon realized that the balloon was caught on the edge of a dark, grumpy-looking grey cloud.

"Oh no," Charlie murmured. He could almost hear the balloon's silent cries for help as it struggled to break free. It was clear that the stubborn grey cloud wasn't about to let it go without a fight.

Without another thought, Charlie looked up at the sky and called, "Nimbus! Nimbus, I need your help!"

A few moments later, Nimbus drifted down from above, his misty form swirling with gentle curiosity. "What's the matter, Charlie?" he asked, following Charlie's gaze toward the balloon.

Charlie pointed. "Look! That little red balloon is stuck, and I think that grey cloud has it trapped."

Nimbus's eyes narrowed as he inspected the scene. "Ah, I see. That's Gloomy, a particularly stubborn cloud who likes to hold onto things, especially bright, cheerful things. It's not easy to get him to let go."

Charlie frowned, determined to help. "Can we talk to him? Maybe if we ask nicely, he'll let the balloon go?"

Nimbus smiled, admiring Charlie's hopefulness. "It's worth a try. Gloomy can be a bit... moody, but sometimes a kind word is all it takes."

With Nimbus at his side, Charlie floated up toward the stubborn grey cloud, watching as it held tightly to the string of the red balloon. The balloon strained and bounced, but Gloomy had it wrapped tightly in his misty grip.

Charlie took a deep breath, steadying his nerves. He floated closer and called out, "Hello, Gloomy!"

The grey cloud turned, his grumpy eyes peering out from the mist. He looked down at Charlie, letting out a low, rumbling sigh. "What do you want, little human?" he grumbled.

Charlie tried his best to smile. "I was wondering if you might let go of that balloon. It looks like it's trying to get home."

Gloomy tightened his grip on the balloon, his eyes narrowing. "This balloon's too bright. It doesn't belong up here with us. I was just keeping it... safe," he muttered, though Charlie could tell there was more to it than that.

Nimbus floated beside Charlie, giving him an encouraging nod. "Go on, Charlie. Keep trying."

Charlie thought for a moment, then softened his voice. "Gloomy, I know you don't mean any harm, but the balloon just wants to float freely. It won't stay long; it just wants to dance in the sky for a little while."

Gloomy gave a small huff, his mist swirling as he glanced down at the bright red balloon in his grip. "I don't like things that are too cheerful," he grumbled, though his voice sounded less harsh. "They don't belong around clouds like me."

Charlie looked at the little balloon, then back at Gloomy, sensing that there was more to the story. "Gloomy, do you feel... lonely up here? Is that why you're holding onto the balloon?"

Gloomy's cloudy form shifted, his eyes softening just a little. "Maybe," he muttered, almost too quietly for Charlie to hear. "Sometimes, it gets lonely being the grey cloud. Everyone loves the bright clouds, the colorful clouds. No one cares about the grey ones."

Charlie's heart went out to him. He floated closer, giving Gloomy a kind look. "I care about you, Gloomy. And so does Nimbus. Every cloud has a place in the sky, even the grey ones. You help make rain for the plants, and you bring calmness when things get too bright. You're important, too."

Nimbus nodded, his voice warm and reassuring. "It's true, Gloomy. Without clouds like you, the sky wouldn't be complete. And I know Charlie's town is grateful for the rain you bring."

Gloomy looked from Nimbus to Charlie, his misty form softening as he took in their words. He looked down at the red balloon, which was still gently tugging at his grip, as if sensing the kindness of Charlie and Nimbus.

After a moment of hesitation, Gloomy sighed. "Alright, little balloon. I'll let you go. But don't go bouncing back up here too soon, you hear?" He gave the balloon one last gentle squeeze before releasing it, watching as it floated freely into the sky.

The red balloon drifted up, bobbing and bouncing joyfully as it rose higher, and Charlie couldn't help but smile. "Thank you, Gloomy," he said, looking at the grey cloud with gratitude. "That was really kind of you."

Gloomy gave a small, reluctant smile, a faint shimmer of light breaking through his grey mist. "Well... I guess it was nice to have a little company, even if just for a moment."

Charlie's face lit up with an idea. "Gloomy, if you ever get lonely, you can always come and join us. You're welcome to float down anytime!"

Gloomy's eyes softened, a hint of warmth breaking through his gruff exterior. "I'll keep that in mind, little human," he said, his voice softer than before. "Maybe I'll stop by sometime."

Nimbus placed a gentle hand on Gloomy's shoulder. "We'd be glad to have you, Gloomy. The sky is big enough for all of us."

With one last look at Charlie and Nimbus, Gloomy gave a low rumble that sounded almost like a purr. Then, with a soft swirl, he floated off into the distance, his grey form drifting peacefully through the sky.

As Charlie and Nimbus watched him go, the red balloon continued its joyful dance, bobbing and twirling through the sky until it was nothing more than a tiny dot in the distance.

Charlie looked at Nimbus, a satisfied smile on his face. "I'm glad Gloomy let go of the balloon. But I think he might've needed it for a moment, just to feel like he wasn't alone."

Nimbus nodded, his eyes filled with pride. "You're right, Charlie. Sometimes even the clouds need a little kindness. You did a wonderful thing today by helping Gloomy see his worth."

Charlie's heart filled with happiness as he looked out over the sky, knowing that he had helped not only the little red balloon but also a lonely grey cloud who just needed a reminder of his own special place.

As they drifted back toward his backyard, Charlie knew he would never look at a grey cloud the same way again. He knew that every cloud, whether bright or grey, had its own role to play, and that kindness could bring light to even the loneliest parts of the sky.

Chapter 12: The Cotton Candy Clouds

One bright afternoon, Charlie was drifting through the sky with Nimbus, watching as the clouds floated lazily by. The air was warm, the sky was clear, and Charlie felt perfectly at peace. Just when he thought the day couldn't get any better, Nimbus turned to him with a mischievous sparkle in his eyes.

"Charlie," Nimbus began with a playful smile, "how would you like to see the sweetest place in the sky?"

Charlie's eyes lit up with curiosity. "The sweetest place? What is it?"

Nimbus winked. "It's a land where clouds aren't just fluffy—they're delicious. Ever heard of the Cotton Candy Clouds?"

Charlie's jaw dropped. "Cotton candy... clouds? You mean, clouds that are actually made of cotton candy?"

"Exactly," Nimbus replied, swirling in excitement. "They're rare and hidden, but if you're up for a little adventure, I think we can find them today."

Charlie felt a burst of excitement. "Yes! Let's go!"

With a nod, Nimbus began to drift higher, and Charlie followed close behind. They floated through soft wisps of mist and passed by big, puffy clouds, going higher and higher until the air began to smell sweet, like sugar and strawberries. Charlie took a deep breath, feeling his mouth water. The scent grew stronger as they went, filling the air with a delicious sweetness.

And then, just as he was wondering if they were close, Charlie saw it—a shimmering pink and blue landscape stretched out before him, soft and fluffy as far as the eye could see. The clouds were swirled with pastel shades of pink, purple, and blue, and they sparkled faintly, like sugar in the sunlight.

"Welcome to the Cotton Candy Clouds," Nimbus announced with a grin, gesturing to the fluffy land around them.

Charlie couldn't believe his eyes. The clouds looked just like real cotton candy, with soft swirls and gentle peaks, each one fluffy and sweet. He reached out and touched one of the clouds, feeling a soft, sugary texture beneath his fingers. To his surprise, it even felt sticky, like real cotton candy!

"Can I... taste it?" Charlie asked, looking over at Nimbus with hopeful eyes.

Nimbus laughed and nodded. "Go ahead! The Cotton Candy Clouds are for tasting and enjoying. Just don't eat too much, or you might float even higher!"

Charlie grinned and carefully pulled off a small piece of the pink cloud in front of him. He took a bite, and his face lit up as the soft, sugary sweetness melted in his mouth. It tasted just like strawberry cotton candy, light and airy, and perfectly sweet.

"This is amazing!" Charlie exclaimed, reaching for another bite.

Nimbus floated beside him, plucking a small piece of blue cloud and tasting it himself. "The flavours change depending on the color. The pink ones are strawberry, the blue ones are blueberry, and the purple ones are grape. Each color has its own delicious taste!"

Charlie's eyes widened with excitement. He drifted over to a purple cloud, pulling off a piece and popping it into his mouth. It tasted just like fresh grapes, sweet and juicy, but with the light, fluffy texture of cotton candy. He laughed in delight, feeling like he was in a sugary dreamland.

They drifted through the cotton candy clouds together, sampling pieces of each color. Charlie tasted the blueberry clouds, which were soft and tangy, and the pale yellow ones, which tasted like lemon drops. He even found a rare orange cloud that tasted like sweet oranges, its flavour bursting on his tongue with every bite.

As they explored, Charlie noticed that the cotton candy clouds formed small hills and valleys, creating a landscape that looked like a sugary paradise. In some places, the clouds had twisted into spirals and peaks, while others were spread out like blankets, soft and inviting.

"This place is incredible," Charlie said, his eyes sparkling as he looked around. "It's like a dream come true!"

Nimbus chuckled. "It's one of the sky's best-kept secrets. The Cotton Candy Clouds only appear on certain days, when the sun is just right. It's a treat for those who believe in the magic of the clouds."

As they floated along, Charlie noticed a small, gentle breeze that made the cotton candy clouds swirl and shift, creating new shapes with every gust. He watched in delight as the clouds formed what looked like a giant castle made of pink and purple spirals, then a field of flowers, each petal made from fluffy cotton candy.

Charlie grinned, feeling a burst of creativity. "Nimbus, can we shape the clouds? Like, make our own cotton candy creations?"

Nimbus's eyes sparkled with excitement. "Of course! Just like when we painted with the wind, you can shape these clouds with your imagination. Try it!"

Charlie reached out, moving his hands through a nearby cloud. The cotton candy mist responded to his touch, swirling and forming shapes as he guided it. He started by making a heart, twisting the pink and blue clouds together until they formed a soft, fluffy heart shape that floated in the air.

Nimbus laughed, clapping his misty hands. "Beautiful, Charlie! Let's make a whole garden of cotton candy shapes!"

With eager hands and a joyful heart, Charlie set to work, shaping the clouds into all sorts of creations. He made cotton candy flowers, soft and sweet, with swirling petals of pink and purple. He created stars that glowed faintly, and even a giant butterfly with wings of blue and yellow that hovered gently in the air.

Nimbus joined in, shaping the clouds into animals—an elephant with a trunk made of pink cotton candy, a giraffe with a long, twisting neck, and even a little puppy that wagged its cotton candy tail.

The two of them laughed and played, filling the sky with their cotton candy creations, each shape drifting softly in the gentle breeze. Charlie felt like he was in a magical candy land, surrounded by sweet, colorful clouds that seemed to come alive with every touch.

After a while, Charlie leaned back, admiring their work. The sky was filled with their cotton candy creations, a landscape of hearts, animals, flowers, and stars, all glowing softly in the sunlight. He felt a deep sense of joy and wonder, grateful for this magical day with Nimbus.

As the sun began to set, casting a warm, golden glow over the cotton candy clouds, Nimbus turned to Charlie with a soft smile. "It's time to head back now, Charlie. The Cotton Candy Clouds are only here for a short time, and they'll fade with the setting sun."

Charlie nodded, feeling a bit sad to leave this sweet paradise but grateful for the magical experience. He took one last look at the cotton candy landscape, the fluffy clouds bathed in the soft light of the sunset.

"Thank you, Nimbus," he said, his voice filled with gratitude. "This was the best adventure yet."

Nimbus nodded, his eyes warm with pride. "I'm glad you enjoyed it, Charlie. The Cotton Candy Clouds are special, and they're even sweeter when shared with a friend."

With one last glance at the cotton candy creations they'd made, Charlie and Nimbus drifted back down toward his backyard. As they touched down on the soft grass, Charlie looked up at the sky, a faint hint of pink and blue still lingering in the clouds above.

He knew he would never forget the taste of the Cotton Candy Clouds or the joy of creating shapes with his hands. And as he looked up at the night sky, he knew that there would always be magic waiting for him in the clouds, sweet and wonderful, just like cotton candy.

Chapter 13: A Whirlwind Friend

One breezy afternoon, Charlie was out in the backyard, lying on the grass and watching the clouds drift by. He was daydreaming about his recent adventures—the Cotton Candy Clouds, the magical Sky Garden, and the firefly clouds that danced at night. Each adventure had introduced him to a new friend or a hidden wonder, and he couldn't help but wonder what else was waiting up there in the sky.

Just as he was thinking about calling Nimbus, he noticed a tiny swirl of dust near his feet. The swirl spun quickly, twisting and whirling, before growing into a small, playful tornado. Charlie's eyes widened in surprise as he watched the mini-tornado spiral around, kicking up bits of grass and dust with each twist and turn.

"Hello!" Charlie called out, waving his hand toward the swirling figure.

The tiny tornado paused, its swirling winds slowing just enough for Charlie to see a small pair of curious eyes peeking out from the center. The little cloud gave a surprised jolt, then spun around in excitement, creating a gentle breeze that tickled Charlie's cheeks.

"Oh, hello!" the tiny tornado said in a breezy, high-pitched voice. "I didn't know anyone could see me down here! My name's Whirly."

"Hi, Whirly!" Charlie said with a warm smile. "I'm Charlie. It's nice to meet you! Are you... are you a little tornado?"

Whirly gave a proud little spin. "Yes, that's right! I'm a tornado, but only a small one." He twisted around, demonstrating his little whirlwind, but it was so gentle that it barely made a leaf rustle. "I'm not like the big tornados that cause storms and thunder. I'm just a tiny little whirl."

Charlie chuckled. "I think you're perfect just the way you are, Whirly."

Whirly's eyes brightened, and he swirled a bit closer, his winds soft and playful. "Thank you, Charlie. But, well... sometimes I wish I could be something else. Something more... gentle."

Charlie tilted his head, curious. "Gentle? Why would you want to be gentle? I thought tornadoes loved to whirl and spin!"

Whirly gave a little sigh, his winds softening as he spoke. "I know. Most tornadoes love to whirl around, but I'm different. I don't want to cause storms or scare anyone. I wish I could just be a gentle breeze, something that makes people smile."

Charlie's heart warmed with sympathy. He could see that Whirly's gentle nature didn't quite fit the whirlwind identity he was born into. "I think that's a wonderful wish, Whirly," Charlie said kindly. "And maybe I can help you make it come true."

Whirly's eyes sparkled with hope. "Really? How?"

Charlie thought for a moment, then smiled. "I think I know someone who can help. Nimbus knows a lot about clouds and the sky. Maybe he can teach you how to be a breeze!"

With excitement twinkling in his eyes, Charlie called up to the sky, "Nimbus! Nimbus, we need your help!"

A moment later, Nimbus drifted down, his misty form shimmering with warmth as he greeted Charlie. "Hello, Charlie! And who's this?" he asked, nodding toward Whirly.

Charlie grinned, introducing his new friend. "Nimbus, this is Whirly. He's a little tornado cloud, but he doesn't want to be a whirlwind. He wants to be a gentle breeze."

Nimbus smiled gently at Whirly, his expression kind and understanding. "Well, Whirly, it's very special to know what you want to be. Not all clouds are meant to be the same. I'd be glad to help you find your gentle side."

Whirly spun in excitement, his winds swirling playfully around Nimbus. "Thank you, Nimbus! I don't want to cause a stir—I just want to make people happy, like a soft breeze on a warm day."

Nimbus nodded, drifting a little higher. "Let's start with something simple, Whirly. Close your eyes, take a deep breath, and feel the air around you. Imagine yourself moving softly, like a feather floating on the wind."

Whirly closed his eyes, concentrating hard as he tried to calm his natural whirlwind energy. His tiny tornado form began to slow, his winds softening and loosening until he looked less like a swirling vortex and more like a gentle puff of mist.

"Good," Nimbus encouraged. "Now, instead of spinning, try moving in a straight line. Think of yourself as a small, gentle breeze, drifting slowly and quietly."

Whirly gave a determined nod, focusing all his energy. He took a deep breath and began to move forward in a smooth, steady motion, his winds as soft as a whisper. He drifted gently, creating a breeze so delicate that it barely rustled the leaves around him.

Charlie's face lit up with joy. "You're doing it, Whirly! You're a gentle breeze!"

Whirly opened his eyes, looking down at himself in amazement. "I did it! I'm not a tornado—I'm a breeze!" He laughed, his voice light and airy as he floated softly through the air, swirling gently around Charlie and Nimbus.

Nimbus smiled, his eyes filled with pride. "See, Whirly? All it took was a bit of focus and a lot of heart. You may have been born a whirlwind, but the sky is big enough for all kinds of clouds. You can be anything you want."

Whirly spun in delight, his winds gentle and soothing. He drifted through the backyard, weaving through the trees and brushing past flowers, his soft breeze leaving a faint scent of fresh air in his wake. He was a new kind of cloud now, one that brought calm instead of chaos, joy instead of thunder.

Charlie clapped his hands, thrilled to see Whirly's transformation. "You're amazing, Whirly! I've never felt a breeze like you before."

Whirly beamed with pride, his gentle winds swirling softly around Charlie. "Thank you, Charlie! Thank you, Nimbus! I never thought I could be a breeze, but now... I feel like I've found who I really am."

Nimbus nodded, placing a gentle hand on Whirly's small form. "Always remember, Whirly, that the sky is filled with all kinds of clouds—big, small, bright, and grey. Each cloud has its own place and purpose. And yours is to bring a gentle, joyful breeze to those who need it."

Whirly's eyes shone with happiness. "I'll be the best breeze I can be! I'll bring smiles and peace wherever I go."

Charlie watched as Whirly floated through the air, a gentle swirl of mist that seemed to carry kindness itself. He knew that his new friend had found his place in the sky, and he felt a warmth in his heart, knowing that he'd been part of Whirly's journey.

As the sun began to set, casting a warm glow over the backyard, Whirly floated over to Charlie one last time, his soft breeze brushing gently against his cheek.

"Thank you, Charlie," Whirly whispered. "You helped me find my true self."

Charlie smiled, his heart full of pride and happiness. "You're welcome, Whirly. I'm so glad we met. The sky is a little brighter with you up there."

With a joyful spin, Whirly drifted back into the sky, his soft winds blending with the evening breeze. As he floated higher, his gentle glow faded into the twilight, leaving a trail of peace and calm in his wake.

And as Charlie watched his friend disappear into the sky, he knew that Whirly would always be there, a gentle breeze bringing quiet joy to the world below.

Chapter 14: The Rainbow River

One bright morning, Nimbus drifted down to Charlie's backyard with a mysterious glint in his eyes, as if he held a magical secret. Charlie looked up eagerly, his curiosity instantly piqued.

"Good morning, Nimbus!" Charlie greeted, smiling up at his cloud friend. "What adventure are we going on today?"

Nimbus chuckled, his misty form shimmering in the morning light. "Today, Charlie, I'm taking you to one of the rarest wonders in the sky—the Rainbow River."

Charlie's eyes widened with excitement. "The Rainbow River? What's that?"

Nimbus smiled, nodding as he began to float upward. "It's exactly what it sounds like—a river made of liquid rainbow. It flows gently through the clouds, filled with colors so bright and beautiful that they seem to come alive. Only a few are lucky enough to see it, but I think today is your day."

Charlie's heart raced as he followed Nimbus up into the sky. The air felt light and fresh, carrying a faint, sweet scent, as if a rainbow had left traces of sugar and flowers behind. As they climbed higher, he noticed that the clouds around them began to shimmer, glowing faintly with hints of color.

Finally, Nimbus slowed and pointed just ahead. "There it is, Charlie—the Rainbow River."

Charlie gasped as he saw it. Flowing smoothly through a cluster of soft white clouds was a river of pure color, winding its way through the sky like a magical stream. The water wasn't clear or blue like ordinary water; instead, it shimmered with every color of the rainbow, shifting from red to orange, yellow to green, blue to violet, and back again. The colors swirled together, blending and separating in a mesmerizing dance of hues.

The river looked alive, its colors flowing like silk ribbons. Sunlight bounced off its surface, making it sparkle like liquid gemstones.

Charlie stared in awe, unable to look away. "It's... it's beautiful," he whispered, hardly able to believe his eyes.

Nimbus nodded, his voice soft with reverence. "The Rainbow River is a rare wonder, Charlie. It's born from the light of the sun and the dreams of the sky. It flows through the clouds, bringing color and magic to the world below."

Charlie felt a surge of excitement and curiosity. "Can I... can I touch it?"

Nimbus gave him an encouraging smile. "Not only can you touch it, but today, you're going to learn to swim in it."

Charlie's eyes went wide with surprise. "Swim? In a rainbow?"

Nimbus chuckled, drifting closer to the river. "Yes, Charlie. The water is light and gentle, just like the clouds. All you need to do is let go of your worries and trust in the magic of the rainbow. The river will carry you."

Charlie took a deep breath, feeling his heart race with anticipation. He floated closer to the edge of the river, looking down at the swirling colors that shimmered beneath him. With a deep breath, he dipped his hand into the water, feeling a soft, warm tingle as his fingers touched the liquid rainbow.

The water felt like silk, smooth and gentle, but with a warmth that made him feel light and happy. Charlie laughed, watching as his hand was coated with a faint shimmer of color, a soft rainbow glow that sparkled in the sunlight.

"Go on, Charlie," Nimbus encouraged, nodding toward the river. "Take the plunge!"

With a grin, Charlie closed his eyes and took a deep breath. Then, without another thought, he leaned forward and slid into the Rainbow River.

The moment he entered the water, he felt a wave of joy wash over him. The river cradled him, its soft currents wrapping around him like a gentle embrace. He opened his eyes and looked down, seeing that his entire body was now glowing with colors—soft reds, bright yellows, and deep blues, all swirling around him like a magical aura.

Charlie laughed in delight, moving his arms and legs, finding that the river lifted him effortlessly. He didn't even need to swim in the usual way; the water seemed to carry him, flowing gently beneath him as he floated along with the current.

Nimbus drifted beside him, his misty form shimmering in the rainbow light. "How does it feel, Charlie?"

Charlie grinned, his eyes sparkling with joy. "It feels amazing! I feel like I'm part of the rainbow!"

The two of them floated down the river together, letting the gentle current carry them. Charlie watched as colors swirled around him, each hue shimmering and shifting, filling the air with a soft, magical glow. He reached out, letting his fingers trail through the water, watching as tiny sparkles of color danced along his skin.

As they drifted along, Nimbus pointed to a spot where the river widened, creating a shallow pool. "This is the Rainbow Pool," he explained. "It's where the colors come together and create patterns. You can even make shapes with your hands."

Charlie's eyes lit up with excitement. He waded into the shallow part of the river, feeling the warmth of the rainbow water around his legs. He cupped his hands, scooping up a handful of the liquid color. As he poured it back into the river, he noticed that he could shape the colors, creating little spirals and waves.

Charlie spent the next few minutes experimenting, creating shapes and patterns in the water. He made a swirling rainbow whirlpool, then a heart that glowed with shades of pink and red. He even formed a small star, which shimmered brightly before blending back into the river.

Nimbus watched, smiling proudly. "You're a natural, Charlie. The Rainbow River responds to those who see its beauty and respect its magic."

Charlie looked up, his heart full of gratitude. "Thank you, Nimbus. This is the most amazing thing I've ever seen."

They floated along in peaceful silence, enjoying the beauty of the Rainbow River. As they rounded a gentle bend, Charlie noticed something extraordinary—a waterfall cascading from a high cloud, spilling liquid rainbow into the river below. The waterfall sparkled with colors, each drop like a tiny jewel, creating a shimmering curtain of light.

Charlie watched in awe as the waterfall flowed into the river, its colors blending seamlessly with the swirling hues below. He swam closer, reaching out to let the rainbow water flow over his hands, feeling the cool, gentle tingle of each drop.

"It's like magic," Charlie whispered, looking up at Nimbus.

Nimbus nodded. "The Rainbow River reminds us of the beauty in every color, in every part of the world. It flows with joy, with dreams, and with light. And today, you are part of it."

Charlie floated there, feeling a deep sense of connection to the river, to the clouds, and to the sky itself. He knew that this was a place he would always carry in his heart, a reminder of the magic and beauty that existed in the world.

As the sun began to dip lower in the sky, casting a warm golden glow over the Rainbow River, Nimbus gently guided Charlie back to the edge. "It's time to head home, Charlie," he said softly.

Charlie nodded, feeling a mixture of joy and gratitude. He climbed out of the river, watching as the colors faded from his skin, leaving a faint, shimmering glow. He looked back at the Rainbow River, the colors still swirling and shining in the evening light.

"Thank you, Nimbus," he said, his voice filled with wonder. "I'll never forget this."

Nimbus placed a gentle misty hand on Charlie's shoulder. "The Rainbow River will always be here, flowing through the clouds, a reminder of the beauty in every color and every dream."

With one last look at the shimmering river, Charlie and Nimbus floated back down to the backyard. As Charlie touched down on the grass, he looked up at the sky, knowing that somewhere above, the Rainbow River was still flowing, carrying magic and color through the clouds.

And as he lay in the grass, watching the evening sky, Charlie felt a warmth in his heart, knowing that he had swum in the Rainbow River—a river of pure magic, beauty, and light.

Chapter 15: Saving the Sunset Clouds

It was late in the afternoon, and Charlie was sitting on the hill behind his house, watching the sky as the colors began to shift toward evening. The sun was low on the horizon, and he eagerly awaited the familiar magic of the sunset clouds—those soft, warm clouds that filled the sky with shades of pink, orange, and gold as the day turned to night.

But something felt... different. As he gazed up at the sky, he noticed that the usual warm colors were missing. The clouds were there, but instead of glowing with their usual fiery brilliance, they looked pale and dull, as if someone had turned off their light.

Charlie frowned, feeling a pang of worry. "What's going on?" he wondered aloud.

Just then, a soft, misty voice called from above. "Charlie!"

He looked up to see Nimbus drifting down, his expression filled with concern.

"Nimbus!" Charlie called, standing up. "Look at the sunset clouds! They're not glowing like they usually do."

Nimbus nodded, looking up at the faded clouds. "Yes, I noticed that too. Something's happened to their glow... it seems that they've lost their colors."

Charlie's heart sank. "But how? The sunset clouds always shine so brightly."

Nimbus floated closer, his eyes filled with worry. "Sunset clouds need the light of the sun to bring out their colors, Charlie. Without it, they fade. And tonight, it seems we're missing an important part—the final sunbeam that lights up the sky."

Charlie's eyes widened. "The sunbeam is missing?"

Nimbus nodded. "It seems to have wandered off somewhere, and without it, the sunset clouds can't glow. We'll need to find it and bring it back before the sun dips too low. Otherwise, the sunset clouds will stay dim, and we'll miss the colors of the evening sky."

CHARLIE AND THE COLOURFUL CLOUDS

Charlie felt a surge of determination. He couldn't let the sunset clouds lose their light. "Let's find the missing sunbeam, Nimbus! We can't let the sunset fade without its colors."

Nimbus gave an approving nod. "Let's go, Charlie. We'll need to search quickly before it's too late."

The two of them floated up into the sky, scanning the horizon for any sign of the missing sunbeam. They drifted through clusters of clouds, calling out softly, hoping the sunbeam might hear them.

"Sunbeam! Where are you?" Charlie called, cupping his hands around his mouth. "The sunset clouds need you!"

They flew over bright patches of sky and through soft layers of mist, but there was no sign of the golden sunbeam anywhere. Charlie's heart began to sink, worried that they might not find it in time.

Just as he was about to give up hope, he spotted a faint, glimmering light on the edge of a distant cloud. It was small and flickering, like a tiny, golden spark that was barely holding on to its glow.

"Nimbus, look!" Charlie pointed, his voice filled with excitement. "There it is!"

They rushed over to the faint light, and as they got closer, Charlie could see that it was indeed the missing sunbeam. It looked tired and a bit dim, as if it had been lost for too long.

Charlie floated up gently, his voice soft and kind. "Hello, little sunbeam. Are you alright?"

The sunbeam looked up, its tiny, golden light flickering weakly. "I... I got lost," it said in a small, trembling voice. "I wandered too far and couldn't find my way back to the sunset clouds."

Nimbus drifted close, his voice warm and reassuring. "It's okay. We're here to help you. The sunset clouds are waiting for you—they need your light to shine."

The sunbeam sighed, its glow fading even more. "I don't know if I have enough light left. I feel so... dim."

Charlie's heart ached for the little sunbeam, and he placed a gentle hand on its soft, glowing form. "Don't worry. We'll help you get back, and I know the sunset clouds will be so happy to see you. Your light is exactly what they need."

The sunbeam seemed to brighten slightly, encouraged by Charlie's words. "You really think so?"

Charlie nodded, smiling. "Absolutely. You have the most beautiful light, and it makes the sunset clouds come to life. Let's get you back where you belong."

With Nimbus's help, they created a gentle breeze to carry the sunbeam, guiding it carefully back toward the sunset clouds. Charlie moved slowly, making sure the little sunbeam stayed safe and steady, offering encouragement with every step of the way.

As they drew closer to the sunset clouds, Charlie could see the clouds growing softer, as if they sensed the approaching light. The sun was hanging low in the sky, casting a dim glow over the landscape. They didn't have much time left.

When they finally reached the edge of the sunset clouds, Charlie turned to the sunbeam, his heart filled with excitement. "This is it! Go on and shine, just like you always do."

The sunbeam looked at Charlie, then took a deep breath. It floated up, releasing a soft, golden light that grew brighter and warmer with each passing second. The sunset clouds seemed to absorb the light, their faded edges beginning to glow with a warm, gentle hue.

Charlie watched in awe as the clouds came back to life, their colors deepening from pale grey to brilliant shades of orange, pink, and gold. The entire sky transformed, as if it had been painted with a giant, glowing brush.

The sunset clouds shimmered and pulsed with color, filling the sky with a breathtaking display of light. The once-dim sunbeam was now shining brighter than ever, its golden glow bringing warmth and beauty to the evening.

Charlie let out a cheer, filled with joy and relief. "You did it, little sunbeam! You brought the sunset clouds back to life!"

The sunbeam twinkled, its light glowing proudly. "Thank you, Charlie. I couldn't have made it back without you."

Nimbus nodded, his eyes filled with pride. "You were wonderful, Charlie. Because of you, the sunset clouds have their glow, and tonight, everyone will see a beautiful sunset."

Charlie looked out at the glowing sky, his heart swelling with happiness. The sunset clouds were as beautiful as ever, filling the horizon with shades of orange, pink, and purple, casting a warm light over the world below.

As they drifted back down toward the earth, Charlie turned to the sunbeam one last time. "Remember, you're important. The sunset wouldn't be the same without you."

The sunbeam gave a soft, golden flicker, its voice warm with gratitude. "Thank you, Charlie. I'll always remember that."

As the sun dipped below the horizon, leaving the sky bathed in twilight, Charlie felt a deep sense of peace. He knew that the sunset clouds would always be there, a reminder of the beauty that even the smallest light could bring.

And as he lay back in the grass, watching the stars begin to twinkle in the sky, Charlie knew that whenever he looked at the sunset, he would remember this day—a day when he saved the sunset clouds and helped a little sunbeam find its way home.

Chapter 16: The Snowflake Puzzle

It was a crisp, chilly afternoon, and Charlie could feel the first hints of winter in the air. The trees were bare, the grass was frosty, and the sky held that pale, silvery glow that hinted at snow. Charlie loved winter, especially when the first snowflakes fell from the sky, blanketing the town in a soft, quiet layer of white.

But as he looked up at the sky, he noticed something strange. Despite the cold, there was no sign of snow. The clouds were gathered in thick layers, but they seemed restless, almost agitated, as if they were struggling to release the winter snow.

Just then, Charlie heard a familiar, breezy voice call down to him. "Charlie!"

He looked up to see Nimbus drifting down, his expression one of concern. "Charlie, we need your help. The snowflake clouds are having trouble, and they can't bring snow to your town until they solve a puzzle."

"A puzzle?" Charlie asked, intrigued.

Nimbus nodded, drifting closer. "The snowflake clouds are made up of intricate patterns, and each snowflake has a unique design. But something's gone wrong, and the patterns are all mixed up. They can't fall as snow until they solve the puzzle and fit the pieces together."

Charlie's eyes widened. "You mean the snowflakes are... like puzzle pieces?"

"Yes," Nimbus replied, his eyes filled with urgency. "Each snowflake has its own special shape, and only when they're in harmony can they come together and drift down as snow. Will you help us solve the Snowflake Puzzle?"

Charlie didn't hesitate. "Of course, Nimbus! Let's go."

With a determined smile, Charlie followed Nimbus up into the sky. The air grew colder as they rose, and soon they found themselves surrounded by thick, fluffy clouds tinged with shades of silver and white. As they drifted closer, Charlie noticed that the clouds were filled with small, glimmering shapes—snowflakes, each one more intricate than the last.

But instead of floating gently, the snowflakes were swirling and tumbling in disarray, their patterns jumbled and chaotic. Charlie could see that some flakes were missing parts, while others had extra bits that didn't fit.

One of the snowflake clouds floated over, its soft, misty form shimmering with a faint, frosty glow. "Oh, thank goodness you're here!" the cloud said, its voice like a whisper of winter wind. "We can't bring snow to the earth until our puzzle is solved. Everything has to fit just right, but we can't seem to get the pieces in order."

Charlie looked at the snowflakes, each one a tiny masterpiece of icy patterns. He could see swirls and stars, delicate branches, and hexagonal shapes, all unique yet somehow connected.

"Don't worry," Charlie said with a reassuring smile. "We'll figure this out together. Let's start by looking at the shapes closely."

Nimbus nodded, guiding Charlie to a cluster of snowflakes that were hovering near the center of the cloud. Each flake was a little different, but Charlie could see that some patterns repeated, like pieces of a larger picture.

"I think some of these are meant to fit together," Charlie murmured, studying the flakes. "Maybe if we match the shapes, we can put the puzzle together."

He reached out, picking up a snowflake with a pointed, star-like pattern. Then he found another snowflake with a similar shape, but it looked like a mirror image. Carefully, he held the two flakes close together, watching as their edges seemed to glow faintly. With a soft shimmer, the flakes locked into place, forming a perfect, symmetrical pattern.

"It worked!" Charlie said, his voice filled with excitement. "These two pieces fit together!"

Nimbus beamed, his misty form swirling with pride. "Great job, Charlie! Keep going. The more pieces we fit, the closer we'll be to bringing snow to the town."

Encouraged by his success, Charlie continued matching the snowflakes, studying each piece carefully. He found flakes with branching shapes that connected like puzzle pieces, their icy edges glowing as they locked into place. Slowly but surely, he began to assemble a pattern that was both intricate and beautiful, a web of frozen stars and delicate lines.

The snowflake cloud watched in awe, its voice soft with gratitude. "You're doing it, Charlie! The puzzle is coming together."

As Charlie worked, he noticed that each time he connected two flakes, a soft, silvery glow spread through the snowflake cloud. It was as if the cloud itself was coming to life, filling with the magic of winter.

Charlie carefully connected another pair of flakes, his eyes lighting up as the final piece fell into place. The entire snowflake puzzle was now complete, an intricate tapestry of patterns that sparkled with frost and light.

The snowflake cloud let out a sigh of relief, its soft voice filled with joy. "Thank you, Charlie. You've solved the puzzle! Now we can finally bring snow to your town."

Charlie watched in wonder as the snowflake cloud began to shimmer, its icy patterns glowing brighter and brighter. One by one, the snowflakes separated, each one retaining its perfect, unique design. They floated gently through the air, drifting in soft spirals as they prepared to fall to the earth.

Nimbus floated beside Charlie, his voice filled with pride. "You did it, Charlie. Thanks to you, the snowflake clouds are ready to bring winter to the world below."

Charlie grinned, his heart brimming with excitement. "Can we watch the snow fall?"

Nimbus smiled. "Of course."

Together, they drifted down through the clouds, watching as the snowflakes began their descent. Each flake twinkled in the light, drifting slowly and gracefully, filling the sky with a cascade of icy patterns. The snowflakes spun and danced as they fell, their delicate designs sparkling like tiny stars.

Charlie looked down, seeing his town below. The rooftops, trees, and streets were soon covered in a soft, powdery layer of white, turning the landscape into a winter wonderland. He could almost hear the joyful shouts of children below, eagerly watching the first snowfall of the season.

As he floated beside Nimbus, Charlie felt a deep sense of satisfaction. He had helped bring winter to his town, and he knew that each snowflake carried a bit of the magic he had unlocked.

The snowflake cloud drifted over, its misty form soft and shimmering. "Thank you, Charlie. Because of you, we can bring joy and beauty to the world below."

Charlie smiled, his heart warm with pride. "It was my pleasure. Snowflakes are amazing—they're like little pieces of art."

Nimbus nodded. "And each one is unique, just like you, Charlie. You brought harmony to the snowflake puzzle, and now winter can unfold in all its beauty."

As they drifted back toward the earth, Charlie looked out at the falling snow, feeling a quiet joy fill his heart. He knew that every snowflake was part of the puzzle he had helped solve, each one carrying a piece of winter magic.

And as he watched the town transform into a world of white, Charlie knew that he would always remember this day—a day when he solved the Snowflake Puzzle and brought the first snowfall to his town.

Chapter 17: A Cloudy Concert

It was a calm evening, and Charlie was lying on the grass, gazing up at the sky as it faded from soft blue to dusky purple. The clouds drifted peacefully above, and everything felt quiet and serene. Just as he was about to close his eyes and relax, he heard a soft, low hum coming from above.

Charlie sat up, listening carefully. The hum was gentle, like a deep note played on a musical instrument, and it seemed to come from the clouds themselves. Intrigued, Charlie stood up and gazed at the sky, trying to locate the source of the sound.

A familiar misty shape floated down from the clouds, his eyes twinkling with excitement.

"Nimbus!" Charlie called, smiling. "Did you hear that sound? It's like the clouds are singing."

Nimbus nodded, his misty form swirling with joy. "You're right, Charlie! Tonight is a special night in the sky—it's the night of the Cloudy Concert!"

Charlie's eyes sparkled with curiosity. "A concert? The clouds are putting on a show?"

Nimbus laughed, giving a playful swirl. "Yes! Once in a while, the clouds gather together to make music. They create a symphony of sounds using the wind, the rain, and even a bit of thunder. It's a celebration of all the sounds of the sky."

Charlie felt a thrill of excitement. "Can I join in?"

Nimbus's eyes twinkled. "Absolutely, Charlie! Tonight, you'll get to play a special instrument made just for you. Come on—I'll show you."

With Nimbus by his side, Charlie floated up into the sky, rising higher and higher until he was surrounded by clouds of all shapes and sizes. The clouds seemed to be buzzing with anticipation, drifting together in small groups, each one preparing for the performance.

Nimbus led Charlie to a small, golden cloud that was shimmering faintly, almost as if it were glowing from within. Lying on top of the cloud was an instrument Charlie had never seen before. It looked like a trumpet, but it was soft and misty, with a long, curved shape that seemed to flow like a gentle breeze.

"This is the Sky Trumpet," Nimbus explained, handing it to Charlie. "It's made from the breath of the wind, and it's used only for the Cloudy Concert. When you play it, it creates a soft, flowing sound that blends with the music of the clouds."

Charlie held the Sky Trumpet carefully, feeling the cool, airy texture of the instrument. He placed his fingers on the soft buttons, feeling a gentle tingle as he held it in his hands. "How do I play it?"

Nimbus smiled. "Just breathe gently into it, and let the sound flow from your heart. The Sky Trumpet responds to your feelings, so think of something beautiful as you play."

Charlie nodded, lifting the trumpet to his lips. He closed his eyes, thinking of the colors of the sunset clouds, the softness of the Rainbow River, and the shimmering light of the firefly clouds. Taking a deep breath, he gently blew into the Sky Trumpet.

A soft, melodic note drifted out, filling the air with a warm, gentle sound that flowed like a breeze. The note rose and fell, creating a soft echo that blended with the hum of the clouds around him. Charlie opened his eyes, smiling in delight.

"You did it, Charlie!" Nimbus cheered. "Your music is perfect for the concert."

Just then, a low, rhythmic beat began to echo from a nearby cloud. Charlie looked over to see a group of thunderclouds creating a soft, rumbling bass line, each one releasing a gentle clap of thunder that sounded like a distant drum. The deep, rolling sounds added a rich layer to the music, filling the sky with a steady, pulsing rhythm.

Next, a group of fluffy cumulus clouds joined in, creating a soft, whooshing sound as they swirled and swayed. Their gentle movements created a flowing melody that blended with the beat of the thunderclouds, creating a soothing harmony.

Charlie lifted the Sky Trumpet to his lips again, playing along with the other clouds. He played soft, high notes that drifted through the air like a gentle breeze, weaving in and out of the other sounds. The music felt alive, flowing through him as he became part of the sky's symphony.

Nimbus floated beside him, his misty form glowing with pride. "You're doing wonderfully, Charlie! Now, let's add a bit of sparkle to the concert."

With a playful twist, Nimbus floated up to a group of small, wispy clouds that shimmered with a faint, silvery light. As they drifted closer, each cloud began to release tiny droplets of rain that sparkled in the moonlight, creating a soft, tinkling sound like wind chimes. The raindrops fell gently, adding a delicate, twinkling melody to the music.

Charlie watched in awe, feeling the beauty of the moment fill his heart. The sky was alive with sound, each cloud adding its unique voice to the concert. He could feel the harmony of the clouds, the rhythm of the thunder, the melody of the breeze, and the sparkling chime of the rain all blending together in perfect unity.

He played his Sky Trumpet, matching his notes to the rhythm of the concert, feeling as though he were part of something larger than himself—a grand, magical symphony that filled the entire sky.

As the music rose to a crescendo, the clouds began to glow, their soft colors lighting up the night like a gentle aurora. The sky was filled with shades of blue, silver, and lavender, each color blending with the music in a beautiful display of light and sound.

Charlie felt a wave of joy and wonder wash over him as he played his final notes, letting the melody drift softly into the night. The other clouds followed suit, their sounds fading gently until only the soft hum of the wind remained, echoing like a lullaby.

CHARLIE AND THE COLOURFUL CLOUDS 73

When the music came to a gentle close, the clouds let out a collective sigh, their misty forms glowing with warmth and happiness. Nimbus floated over to Charlie, his eyes filled with pride.

"You were wonderful, Charlie. The clouds were thrilled to have you join the concert. You added a special magic to the music tonight."

Charlie lowered the Sky Trumpet, his heart full of gratitude. "Thank you, Nimbus. That was the most amazing experience. I felt like I was part of the sky."

Nimbus placed a gentle hand on Charlie's shoulder. "You are part of the sky, Charlie. You've always belonged here, and tonight, you became one with its music."

As they floated back down to the earth, Charlie held the Sky Trumpet close, feeling its soft, misty texture as a reminder of the night's magic. He knew he would always remember the Cloudy Concert, a night when he became part of a symphony of clouds, rain, thunder, and wind.

As he touched down on the grass and looked up at the quiet, star-filled sky, Charlie felt a sense of peace. He knew that the music of the clouds was always there, waiting to be heard by those who believed.

And as he drifted off to sleep, he could still hear the faint, gentle notes of the Cloudy Concert, filling his dreams with the sound of the sky's soft, beautiful song.

Chapter 18: The Disappearing Clouds

Charlie was out in the backyard one sunny afternoon, looking up at the sky and hoping to see his friends—the colorful clouds that had brought him so much wonder and joy. But as he scanned the sky, he noticed something strange. The usually vibrant clouds, filled with shades of pink, blue, and gold, seemed faded, almost transparent, like they were slowly disappearing.

A pang of worry struck his heart. He had never seen the colorful clouds look so faint, and he couldn't imagine a sky without them. He knew something had to be wrong, and he had to figure out what was happening before it was too late.

Just then, a familiar misty shape drifted down beside him. Nimbus looked more serious than Charlie had ever seen him.

"Nimbus!" Charlie called, running over. "The colorful clouds—they're fading! What's happening to them?"

Nimbus sighed, his misty form swirling with concern. "Yes, Charlie. The clouds are losing their color, and if we don't find out why, they may disappear entirely."

Charlie's heart sank. "But why? The clouds have always been full of color and life."

Nimbus looked at him, his eyes filled with a mixture of worry and hope. "The colorful clouds draw their strength from the wonder and imagination of the people below. When people look up with joy, awe, and curiosity, the clouds are able to keep their colors bright and vibrant. But lately, fewer people have been looking up, and the clouds have started to fade."

Charlie thought about this, feeling a deep sadness for the colorful clouds. "People aren't looking up?" he asked, puzzled.

Nimbus nodded. "Yes, many people have become busy and distracted. They've forgotten to pause and look up at the beauty of the sky. Without those moments of wonder, the colorful clouds can't keep their glow."

Charlie's mind raced as he thought of all the times he had looked up at the clouds, feeling amazed and inspired by their colors and shapes. He realized how important it was to appreciate the sky, to see the magic in the clouds and let that joy fill his heart. But now, he needed to remind others to do the same.

"We have to save them, Nimbus!" Charlie said, determination shining in his eyes. "There has to be a way to bring the colors back."

Nimbus's eyes softened with hope. "There is a way, Charlie, but it will take a lot of belief and a lot of love for the sky. We need to rekindle that sense of wonder in the people below. If they start looking up again, even just for a moment, it could be enough to restore the clouds' colors."

Charlie felt a spark of excitement. He knew he couldn't do it alone, but he could help inspire others. "I have an idea, Nimbus. Let's put on a show in the sky! If we create something amazing, something so beautiful that people can't help but look up, maybe it will remind them of the magic in the clouds."

Nimbus's eyes lit up with a renewed sense of purpose. "That's a wonderful idea, Charlie. The clouds and I will help create the most colorful display the sky has ever seen."

With Nimbus's guidance, Charlie floated up into the sky, gathering the remaining colorful clouds. He explained his plan, and each cloud nodded, their faint colors brightening slightly at the thought of bringing wonder back to the people below.

They started by arranging the clouds in layers, creating soft, swirling patterns that looked like a giant painting in the sky. Nimbus floated nearby, guiding each cloud with gentle gusts of wind, helping them create intricate shapes and patterns.

Then, Charlie had an idea to make the display even more breathtaking. "Let's add a rainbow mist!" he suggested, remembering the magical colors of the Rainbow River.

Nimbus nodded, summoning a few rainbow clouds that still held a faint shimmer. They floated over, releasing a gentle, colorful mist that drifted through the patterns, adding swirls of red, orange, green, and blue to the display. The mist sparkled in the sunlight, creating a soft glow that made the clouds look like they were painted with light.

As they worked, Charlie noticed a few people below stopping to look up. A child tugged at her mother's hand, pointing at the sky with wide eyes. A group of friends paused in their conversation, looking up with awe as the colors swirled and danced above them.

Charlie felt his heart lift as he saw the expressions of wonder on their faces. He could feel the clouds responding, their colors growing stronger, as if they were drawing energy from each person's gaze.

But they needed more.

Charlie had one last idea, and he turned to Nimbus with a hopeful smile. "Do you think we could make a giant rainbow in the sky? One that stretches all the way across the horizon?"

Nimbus's eyes sparkled with excitement. "Yes, Charlie! The clouds are ready. Let's bring the rainbow to life."

Together, they gathered the remaining colorful clouds, arranging them in a sweeping arc that stretched from one end of the sky to the other. The rainbow mist filled the space, blending each color together in perfect harmony. When they were ready, Nimbus gave a soft command, and the clouds released a gentle, glowing light.

A brilliant rainbow appeared, filling the sky with vibrant colors that seemed to shimmer and pulse with life. The rainbow arced gracefully across the sky, glowing with a magical intensity that made the entire horizon sparkle. It was so bright and beautiful that even people inside their homes stopped to look out their windows, drawn by the rainbow's glow.

Below, the town came alive with gasps of amazement and joy. People gathered in the streets, on rooftops, and in parks, pointing at the sky and watching in wonder as the clouds and rainbow filled the sky with color.

Charlie felt a warmth fill his heart as he saw more and more people looking up, their faces filled with awe. The clouds seemed to respond, their colors growing richer and brighter with each gaze. The fading clouds regained their brilliance, glowing with renewed life, as if they had been reawakened by the love and wonder of the people below.

As the display reached its peak, the clouds came together in one final flourish, creating a breathtaking scene that filled the entire sky. Then, slowly, they began to drift apart, their colors still strong and vibrant, no longer fading.

Nimbus floated over to Charlie, his eyes filled with gratitude. "You did it, Charlie. You brought the colors back. The clouds are alive with wonder again."

Charlie smiled, feeling a deep sense of joy and fulfilment. "I couldn't have done it without you, Nimbus. We reminded everyone to look up and see the magic in the sky."

As they drifted back down to the earth, Charlie looked up at the colorful clouds, knowing they would continue to glow as long as people took the time to appreciate their beauty. He felt proud to have been part of such a special moment, one that brought joy and wonder to everyone who looked up.

And as he lay back on the grass, watching the colorful clouds drift across the sky, Charlie knew that he would always carry the magic of this day in his heart—a day when he saved the colorful clouds by helping people remember the beauty of the world above.

Chapter 19: The Great Cloud Chase

It was late afternoon, and Charlie was sitting on his favorite hill, waiting for the sunset. He loved this time of day, when the sky filled with warm, glowing colors. But today, something was wrong. The sun was beginning to dip toward the horizon, but the usual shades of pink, orange, and gold were nowhere to be seen. Instead, the sky was an ordinary, pale blue, with only a few faded clouds drifting along.

Charlie's heart sank. Without the sunset colors, the evening sky looked empty, missing the magic that made it come alive.

Just then, he spotted a familiar misty figure gliding down from the sky. Nimbus floated over, his expression filled with concern.

"Nimbus!" Charlie called, hurrying over. "What happened to the sunset colors?"

Nimbus shook his head, a worried look in his eyes. "It's a disaster, Charlie. A cloud named Flicker has stolen the colors of the sunset. He grabbed them all and is racing through the sky, refusing to give them back."

Charlie's eyes widened in surprise. "A cloud stole the sunset colors? But why?"

Nimbus sighed. "Flicker is a mischievous cloud. He loves attention, and he thinks that if he keeps all the colors to himself, he'll be the brightest, most beautiful cloud in the sky. But what he doesn't realize is that without the sunset colors, the evening will feel empty."

Charlie felt a spark of determination. "We have to get those colors back! The sunset is too important to lose."

Nimbus nodded. "Agreed. We'll need to chase Flicker down and convince him to return the colors before the sun sets completely. If we don't, there won't be a sunset tonight."

With a determined grin, Charlie climbed onto Nimbus, and together, they soared up into the sky, rising higher as they scanned the horizon for any sign of Flicker.

As they flew, Charlie spotted a glimmer of color on the edge of a distant cloud bank. "There!" he shouted, pointing to a bright flash of pink and orange streaking across the sky. "That must be Flicker!"

They zoomed toward the colorful streak, and soon, Charlie could see Flicker clearly—a small, puffy cloud glowing with stolen shades of pink, orange, purple, and gold. Flicker looked like he was wearing the sunset, shimmering with colors that weren't his own.

"Flicker!" Nimbus called out, his voice firm. "You need to give back the sunset colors. They belong to the whole sky, not just to you."

Flicker turned, a mischievous grin on his misty face. "Why should I? Look at me—I'm the brightest cloud in the sky! I'm the star of the sunset now."

Charlie floated forward, trying to reason with the stubborn cloud. "But Flicker, the sunset is meant for everyone to enjoy. When you keep the colors to yourself, the rest of the sky misses out. Don't you want everyone to see how beautiful it can be?"

Flicker hesitated, glancing around as if he were considering Charlie's words. But then he shook his head. "I like being special. If I give up the colors, I'll just be a regular cloud again."

Nimbus sighed, realizing that Flicker needed a little more convincing. "Flicker, being part of the sunset makes you special in a different way. When you share the colors, you help create something magical that everyone can see. You'll still shine, but so will the whole sky."

Flicker looked uncertain, his colors flickering slightly as he thought about it. "But... I want to be the brightest."

Charlie thought quickly, trying to find a way to help Flicker understand. "What if we let you lead the sunset?" he suggested. "You can be the first cloud in the sky to glow with the colors, and all the other clouds will follow your lead. You'll be the star of the show!"

Flicker's eyes sparkled with excitement. "I get to lead the sunset?"

Charlie nodded. "Yes! You'll be the first cloud everyone sees, and you'll guide the colors across the sky."

Flicker looked down at his stolen colors, a faint smile on his misty face. "Alright," he said finally, his voice softer. "I'll share the colors... as long as I get to lead."

Charlie and Nimbus let out sighs of relief. "Thank you, Flicker," Nimbus said warmly. "You're doing something wonderful for everyone."

Slowly, Flicker began to release the colors he'd gathered, sending soft tendrils of pink and orange drifting across the sky. As the colors spread, they touched the other clouds, bringing them to life with warm, glowing shades. Soon, the entire sky was filled with vibrant hues, each cloud shimmering with a piece of the sunset.

Charlie watched in awe as Flicker floated to the front of the sunset, leading the colors in a graceful arc across the horizon. Flicker's misty form glowed with pride, shining brightly as he guided the other clouds, just as Charlie had promised.

With Flicker leading the way, the sunset became a breathtaking display, the colors blending together in a soft, radiant glow that stretched from one end of the sky to the other. People below looked up, gasping in wonder as the sky transformed into a sea of colors, filling the evening with beauty and warmth.

Charlie smiled, feeling a deep sense of joy and accomplishment. Flicker had learned the value of sharing, and the sunset was more beautiful than ever.

As the last rays of light faded and the colors slowly melted into twilight, Flicker drifted over to Charlie, his eyes bright with gratitude.

"Thank you, Charlie," Flicker said quietly. "You were right. Leading the sunset was even better than keeping the colors to myself. I feel... like I was part of something bigger."

Charlie grinned. "You were, Flicker. The sunset needs every cloud to make it beautiful, and you helped make it happen."

Nimbus drifted beside them, his eyes filled with pride. "Tonight was a perfect sunset, thanks to all of you."

As they floated back down to the ground, Charlie looked up at Flicker, knowing that he'd made a new friend in the mischievous cloud. Flicker gave him a final nod of gratitude, then drifted off into the night, a soft glow still lingering on his misty form.

As Charlie lay back on the grass, watching the stars come out, he felt a deep sense of peace. He knew that every sunset was a reminder of the beauty that could be created when everyone shared a piece of their light.

And as he closed his eyes, he carried the colors of the sunset in his heart, a memory of the Great Cloud Chase and the lesson of a little cloud who learned the magic of giving.

Chapter 20: Learning to Share the Sky

It was a warm afternoon, and Charlie was relaxing in his backyard, watching the clouds drift lazily across the sky. The air was calm, and everything felt peaceful. But then, out of nowhere, a loud rumble echoed from above, and a dark, towering cloud rolled into view, grumbling and crackling with small bursts of lightning.

Charlie recognized that rumble immediately. "Oh no," he muttered with a grin, standing up. "It's Thunder!"

Sure enough, Thunder the storm cloud was back, filling the sky with his moody, swirling presence. He was much larger than the other clouds around him, his misty form crackling with energy as he took up more and more space in the sky. The smaller clouds scattered, moving to the edges to avoid getting caught in Thunder's gusty winds.

Nimbus floated down to Charlie, his expression both amused and a little concerned. "Hello, Charlie. It seems Thunder's back, and he's taking up... quite a bit of room."

Charlie sighed. "He does like to be the center of attention, doesn't he?"

Nimbus nodded, watching as Thunder let out another loud rumble, his clouds swirling with dramatic dark shades of grey and silver. "Yes, Thunder has a big personality, and he loves to show off. But he needs to learn that there's enough sky for everyone. The other clouds would love to be part of the day too, but Thunder's making it hard for them."

Charlie thought about it, then nodded. "Maybe we can help him understand. Thunder's powerful, but maybe he just needs a little reminder that sharing makes the sky better for everyone."

Nimbus smiled at Charlie's determination. "Good idea, Charlie. Let's go talk to him."

Together, they floated up toward Thunder, who was grumbling loudly and puffing out his stormy chest, sending small bursts of thunder and lightning through the sky.

"Hey, Thunder!" Charlie called out, waving his hand.

Thunder turned, looking down at Charlie and Nimbus with a small smirk. "Well, well, look who's here," he boomed. "Come to watch the Thunder Show, have you? I'm giving the sky some excitement!"

Charlie floated closer, smiling gently. "You're definitely exciting, Thunder. But don't you think you're taking up a lot of space? The other clouds might want to be part of the sky too."

Thunder huffed, sending out a small rumble of thunder. "Why should I share? I'm the biggest and loudest! I'm the storm cloud—the one everyone notices!"

Charlie nodded thoughtfully. "It's true—you are strong and powerful. But there's room in the sky for everyone, Thunder. When you take up all the space, the other clouds miss out on being part of the day."

Thunder looked around at the smaller clouds, who were hovering quietly at the edges, their soft, pastel colors barely visible beside Thunder's dark, swirling presence.

"But... they're so small and quiet," Thunder muttered, sounding slightly unsure. "I bring excitement to the sky. I make people look up."

Nimbus floated closer, his voice gentle. "Thunder, excitement is important, but so is balance. The sky needs a little bit of everything—sunshine, calm clouds, and even your thunder. When everyone shares, the sky becomes more beautiful."

Thunder looked thoughtful, watching as a few wispy clouds drifted cautiously closer, as if they were hoping he'd give them space.

Charlie took a deep breath, then spoke up. "Thunder, why don't we try something different today? You could take turns with the other clouds, sharing the sky so everyone has a chance to shine. You'd still have your moment, but so would they. It might make the day even better."

Thunder hesitated, looking uncertain. He glanced at the other clouds, then back at Charlie. "Take turns?" he muttered, sounding like the idea was entirely new to him.

Charlie nodded, smiling. "Yes! Imagine the sky like a big, beautiful stage. You could have your time to rumble and show off, and then the other clouds could have their peaceful moments. That way, people get to enjoy everything the sky has to offer."

Thunder grumbled a little, but his voice was softer. "I suppose... I could give it a try. Just this once."

Charlie and Nimbus exchanged a hopeful smile, then backed up a little to give Thunder room to start.

With a deep, booming rumble, Thunder floated to the center of the sky, his dark clouds swirling as he released a few dramatic claps of thunder. A gentle flash of lightning lit up his cloud, creating a thrilling show that made the other clouds shiver in excitement. People below looked up, admiring the powerful display, some even clapping their hands in awe.

After a few minutes, Thunder gave one last clap of thunder, then floated to the side, looking over at the other clouds. "Alright, then. Your turn," he said, sounding a bit reluctant but also curious.

A small, fluffy cumulus cloud floated forward, glowing softly as it took its place in the sky. The cloud spread out, filling the air with a soft, golden light that cast a warm, calming glow over the town below. People looked up, smiling at the peaceful sight, feeling the soothing effect of the gentle cloud.

Charlie looked over at Thunder, who was watching the cumulus cloud with a mix of surprise and admiration. "See, Thunder?" Charlie said. "The sky needs your strength and their softness. When you share, it makes everything more beautiful."

Thunder nodded slowly, his dark form softening a bit. "I... I suppose it is nice to see them out there," he admitted, almost reluctantly. "They do add something."

Nimbus smiled. "Yes, Thunder. And together, you all create a balanced, beautiful sky. Every cloud has a place, even you."

With newfound understanding, Thunder joined the other clouds, taking his place in a smaller part of the sky, but still standing out with his powerful, stormy presence. As he shared the space with the others, he noticed that the sky looked fuller and more vibrant, with each cloud adding its own unique touch.

Throughout the day, Thunder and the other clouds took turns, each one bringing a different feeling to the sky. Thunder would rumble for a few minutes, adding a thrilling energy, and then he'd step aside to let the softer, fluffier clouds take over, bringing calm and warmth to the day.

By evening, Thunder had settled into his role, enjoying the harmony of the shared sky. When the sunset clouds appeared, filling the sky with colors of pink, orange, and purple, Thunder watched in awe, realizing that the sky was even more beautiful with everyone's contributions.

As the sun dipped below the horizon, Thunder floated over to Charlie, his voice quieter and more thoughtful than usual. "Thank you, Charlie," he said. "I never realized how much better the sky could be when I shared it."

Charlie smiled, his heart warm with pride. "You did great, Thunder. The sky needs all of you to be its best. Sharing makes everything more special."

Nimbus nodded in agreement. "Tonight was one of the most beautiful skies I've seen in a long time. You all made it happen—together."

Thunder gave a soft rumble of appreciation, his stormy form glowing faintly as he drifted beside the other clouds, finally content to be part of the sky rather than the center of it.

As Charlie watched the evening settle in, he felt a deep sense of peace. He knew that Thunder had learned an important lesson about sharing, one that would make the sky a better, more balanced place for everyone.

And as he lay back in the grass, gazing up at the stars that began to twinkle in the night, Charlie knew that each cloud—whether big, small, bright, or stormy—had its own role to play, creating a sky that was complete and beautiful for all.

Chapter 21: The Day of the Dull Gray Clouds

Charlie woke up one morning to find the sky looking strange and unusually dull. Instead of the usual bright, fluffy clouds floating cheerfully above, the entire sky was blanketed in a flat, grey sheet that stretched from one end of the horizon to the other. Every cloud looked the same—plain, dull grey, without a hint of color or sparkle.

Charlie rubbed his eyes, thinking it must be some kind of early morning fog, but as the day wore on, the grey clouds stayed exactly where they were, showing no sign of shifting or brightening.

"Where are all the colors?" Charlie wondered aloud, feeling a pang of worry. The sky felt lifeless and flat without its usual vibrancy, and the whole day seemed a little dimmer because of it.

Just then, a familiar misty shape floated down from the grey expanse above. Nimbus, his cheerful cloud friend, looked as concerned as Charlie felt.

"Nimbus!" Charlie called out, running over to him. "What's going on with the sky? Why are all the clouds grey?"

Nimbus sighed, his usually bright form looking dull and washed out. "It's not just the sky, Charlie. All the clouds have lost their colors. It's as if the joy and light that usually fill the clouds have disappeared."

Charlie's heart sank. "But... why? What could have happened to make everything so grey?"

Nimbus looked down thoughtfully, his voice soft. "The clouds get their colors from feelings—joy, imagination, hope. On days when people are filled with happiness or wonder, the colors shine brightly. But sometimes, when there's too much worry, sadness, or distraction below, the clouds lose their brightness and turn grey."

Charlie felt a wave of determination. He couldn't let the sky stay like this. The colorful clouds brought magic and happiness to the world, and he knew he had to do something to bring the colors back.

"We have to help the clouds find their colors again," Charlie said, looking up at Nimbus with resolve. "Is there a way we can bring back the joy and wonder they need?"

Nimbus nodded, a glimmer of hope in his eyes. "There might be. The clouds respond to the feelings of those who look up to them. If we can create something joyful or inspiring, something that makes people look up and feel happy, the clouds might find their colors again."

Charlie thought about all the things that had brought color to the sky before—the rainbow mists, the vibrant sunsets, the dances of the firefly clouds. He realized that he needed to create something big and beautiful, something so full of wonder that people would feel the magic in their hearts.

A smile spread across Charlie's face as an idea began to form. "What if we put on a show in the sky? A display of shapes and colors that everyone can see?"

Nimbus's eyes lit up. "That's a wonderful idea, Charlie! We can use the clouds to create shapes, just like when you painted in the sky before. This time, we'll make it even bigger, something people will remember."

Charlie climbed onto Nimbus's misty form, and together, they floated up into the dull grey sky. The air felt heavy and quiet, and as Charlie looked around, he could see that every cloud was covered in a dim layer of grey mist, as if they were weighed down by the lack of color.

"Alright, let's start with something simple to catch people's attention," Charlie suggested, thinking carefully. "How about we make a giant heart in the sky?"

Nimbus smiled, nodding in agreement. "A heart it is!"

Charlie reached out to the nearest grey cloud, concentrating as he shaped it with his hands. Slowly, the cloud began to take form, its edges softening into the rounded curves of a heart. As he worked, he thought of all the love and kindness he wanted to send to the people below, imagining the heart filled with warmth and care.

Gradually, the cloud heart started to brighten, a faint pinkish glow beginning to emerge from within the grey mist. Nimbus and Charlie exchanged a hopeful glance, encouraged by the first hint of color breaking through.

Next, Charlie and Nimbus shaped another cloud into a smiling face, adding bright, round eyes and a wide grin. As they smoothed the edges, thinking of laughter and joy, the cloud began to glow with a soft golden hue, as if it were smiling down at the world below.

People began to notice. Charlie could see them pointing up, their faces lighting up with surprise and delight as they watched the shapes form in the sky.

"Let's make some animals," Charlie suggested, grinning. "People love animals!"

Together, they crafted a fluffy bunny cloud with long ears, a playful cat with a curly tail, and a giant bird soaring across the sky with wings spread wide. Each time they completed a shape, the grey mist faded a little more, revealing soft colors that shone with warmth and joy.

The more they worked, the brighter the clouds became. Charlie could feel the excitement building below as people gathered to watch the display. Some were smiling, others laughing and pointing, and Charlie even saw a few children jumping up and down, their eyes filled with wonder.

As the joy spread, the clouds around them began to shimmer, their grey layers melting away to reveal shades of pink, blue, yellow, and purple. It was as if the sky itself were waking up, coming back to life with every smile and every gaze from below.

To finish their display, Nimbus had an idea. "Let's create a rainbow arc across the sky to tie it all together."

Charlie's face lit up. "Yes! A rainbow is perfect!"

They gathered the remaining clouds, arranging them in a sweeping arc that stretched across the entire horizon. Nimbus released a soft, colorful mist that filled the arc with vibrant hues, blending from red to violet in a stunning display.

As the rainbow appeared, a collective gasp rose from the people below. The whole town stopped to look, their eyes wide with awe as the colorful clouds filled the sky, shining with the magic of joy and wonder.

The clouds, now vibrant and alive, glowed brightly in response to the happiness below. The sky was no longer dull and grey—it was filled with colors that sparkled in the sunlight, each one more vivid than the last.

Nimbus floated beside Charlie, his eyes filled with pride. "You did it, Charlie. You brought the colors back to the sky. Today, you reminded everyone of the beauty above them."

Charlie looked down at the people below, his heart swelling with pride. "It wasn't just me, Nimbus. It was everyone. The joy and wonder they felt brought the colors back. The clouds came to life because people believed in the magic of the sky."

As they drifted back down to earth, Charlie took one last look at the colorful clouds, feeling a deep sense of peace. He knew that the magic of the sky was always there, waiting to be seen by those who looked up with open hearts.

And as he lay back on the grass, watching the vibrant display above, Charlie felt a warmth in his heart, knowing that even on the dullest days, a little bit of joy and wonder could bring color back to the world.

Chapter 22: The Cloud Maze

One afternoon, Charlie was floating through the sky with Nimbus, admiring the soft shapes and patterns of the clouds around him. They had drifted higher than usual, exploring new parts of the sky that Charlie hadn't seen before. The clouds here were thick and swirling, creating walls of mist that rose up like towers, shifting and moving with the breeze.

"Wow, this part of the sky is amazing," Charlie said, looking around in awe.

Nimbus chuckled. "Yes, Charlie. You're in the maze of clouds—a place where the mist forms intricate paths and hidden passageways. It's a favorite spot for clouds who like a little adventure."

Charlie's eyes lit up with excitement. "A maze? That sounds fun! Can we explore it?"

Nimbus nodded, smiling. "Of course. But be careful—the Cloud Maze is known for changing shape, and it's easy to get turned around."

Charlie wasn't worried. "I'll be careful," he promised, already eager to begin.

With a playful grin, Charlie drifted into the maze, marveling at the way the clouds shifted around him. The walls of the maze were thick and soft, made of swirling mist that seemed to glow faintly in the sunlight. The paths twisted and turned, forming narrow passages and wide openings, each one inviting him to explore further.

As he moved deeper into the maze, Charlie noticed that the air grew cooler and quieter. He couldn't hear the usual hum of the wind or Nimbus's soft voice. It was just him and the misty paths, winding and twisting in every direction.

Charlie took a left turn, then a right, and then another left, following the paths that seemed to call to him. But after a few minutes, he realized that everything looked the same. Each passage seemed to lead to another, identical one, and he couldn't see an exit anywhere.

He stopped, looking around with a mix of excitement and uncertainty. "Nimbus?" he called out, hoping his friend was nearby. But there was no answer—just the soft, swirling mist around him.

Charlie took a deep breath, reminding himself to stay calm. He had explored plenty of cloud formations before, and he was confident he could find his way out. But as he moved forward, he noticed that the walls seemed to shift each time he turned. It was as if the maze were alive, changing shape with every step he took.

After a few more turns, Charlie found himself in a dead end—a small, circular clearing surrounded by thick, swirling mist. He looked around, realizing he was truly lost. For the first time, he felt a pang of worry.

"Think, Charlie," he told himself, taking a calming breath. "There has to be a way out. You just need to find it."

He looked up, hoping to see the sky above, but the mist was so thick that it obscured everything. It was like being in a world made entirely of clouds, with no landmarks to guide him.

Just then, he remembered something Nimbus had taught him: The clouds respond to feelings and intentions. If you're calm and focused, they'll guide you where you need to go.

Charlie closed his eyes, letting go of his worry. He took a deep breath, clearing his mind and focusing on the feeling of peace and trust. He pictured himself finding the way out, feeling the warmth of the sun on his face as he escaped the maze.

When he opened his eyes, he noticed that the mist had softened, parting slightly to reveal a narrow path leading to the right.

Charlie smiled, feeling a surge of hope. "Thank you, clouds," he whispered, taking a step toward the new path.

He followed the path, moving carefully and staying focused on his sense of calm. Each time he encountered a dead end, he would pause, clear his mind, and refocus. And each time, the clouds would part slightly, showing him a new path forward.

As he moved deeper into the maze, he began to notice subtle hints—tiny sparkles in the mist, faint glimmers of light that seemed to guide him. He followed the sparkles, letting them lead him through twists and turns, feeling more confident with each step.

Finally, after what felt like a long journey, Charlie saw a faint glow ahead. He quickened his pace, his heart pounding with excitement. The misty walls began to thin, and soon he found himself stepping into an open clearing bathed in warm sunlight.

He looked around, realizing he was at the edge of the maze. He had made it out!

Just as he was about to celebrate, Nimbus drifted down, his eyes filled with relief. "Charlie! You found your way out!"

Charlie grinned, his heart swelling with pride. "I did! The maze was tricky, but I stayed calm, and the clouds showed me the way."

Nimbus nodded, a proud smile on his face. "The Cloud Maze is a place that teaches patience and trust. You learned how to find your way by listening to your instincts and letting the clouds guide you."

Charlie looked back at the maze, feeling a mix of respect and gratitude. "It was amazing, Nimbus. I was scared at first, but then I realized that the clouds were there to help me. I just had to be calm and trust them."

Nimbus placed a gentle hand on Charlie's shoulder. "The sky is full of mystery and adventure, Charlie, but it's also filled with guidance. Whenever you're lost, remember to trust yourself and the clouds. They'll always help you find your way."

As they floated back down to the ground, Charlie took one last look at the Cloud Maze, feeling a newfound sense of confidence. He knew that even when things felt confusing or uncertain, he had the strength and calm within him to find his way.

And as he lay back in the grass, gazing up at the ever-shifting clouds, he knew that every adventure—no matter how puzzling—would lead him to new understanding, as long as he stayed calm and trusted himself.

Chapter 23: A Storm of Emotions

One morning, Charlie woke up feeling a swirl of emotions he couldn't quite put into words. His mind was a jumble of thoughts, and his heart felt heavy. He had woken up from a strange dream, and he wasn't sure why, but he felt restless, anxious, and a little sad. The feeling seemed to follow him as he got ready for the day, clouding his mind like a grey haze.

As he stepped outside, hoping the fresh air might make him feel better, he looked up and noticed that the sky was unusually dark and turbulent. Thick, swirling clouds were gathering overhead, their shades of grey and deep blue shifting like waves in a stormy sea.

"Nimbus?" Charlie called, wondering if his friend was somewhere nearby.

A moment later, Nimbus floated down, his misty form looking unsettled. "Hello, Charlie. Are you... feeling alright?" he asked, his eyes full of gentle concern.

Charlie sighed, shrugging his shoulders. "I don't know. I feel... weird. Sad and a bit worried, but I'm not sure why."

Nimbus looked around at the churning sky, then back at Charlie. "The clouds are reacting to your feelings, Charlie. When you're calm and happy, the sky reflects that. But when your emotions are intense, they can create a storm. Today, it looks like your feelings are creating a bit of chaos."

Charlie stared up at the sky, watching as the dark clouds grew thicker, lightning crackling faintly within them. He realized that the storm he was seeing wasn't just any storm—it was his storm, created by his own emotions.

Charlie felt a pang of guilt. "I didn't mean to make the clouds upset. I just can't seem to calm down. Everything feels out of control."

Nimbus floated closer, his eyes filled with understanding. "It's okay, Charlie. Everyone has stormy days. Sometimes our feelings become too big to hold inside, and they need a way to release. The important thing is learning how to calm the storm."

Charlie took a deep breath, nodding slowly. "But how? I don't know if I can stop feeling this way."

Nimbus thought for a moment, then gently placed a misty hand on Charlie's shoulder. "Let's go up into the sky together. I'll guide you, and we'll calm the storm one step at a time."

Charlie climbed onto Nimbus, and together they floated up into the swirling clouds. As they rose higher, the wind picked up, whipping around them with gusts that seemed to echo his own restlessness. Thunder rumbled softly, and Charlie felt the tension within him grow even stronger.

Nimbus's voice broke through his thoughts, gentle yet steady. "Close your eyes, Charlie, and take a deep breath. Imagine yourself holding onto your feelings like clouds in the sky."

Charlie closed his eyes, taking a deep breath. He pictured each feeling as a cloud around him—his worry, his sadness, his frustration. Each emotion formed a misty shape in his mind, swirling and changing as he acknowledged them.

"Now, one by one, let each cloud drift away," Nimbus continued softly. "Take a deep breath, and as you exhale, imagine releasing each feeling, letting it float away into the sky."

Charlie took another deep breath, imagining his worry as a dark, heavy cloud. As he exhaled, he pictured it lifting up, becoming lighter and softer, drifting away into the distance.

He continued with each feeling, naming them silently in his mind and releasing them with each breath. His sadness lifted, softening into a gentle mist that faded into the sky. His frustration drifted up, breaking apart like a dissolving storm cloud.

As he continued, he felt a strange sense of peace washing over him, like a gentle rain clearing the air after a long storm. The thunder quieted, and the wind began to calm, the heavy clouds around him softening into a gentle grey.

When Charlie opened his eyes, he saw that the sky had changed. The storm clouds were no longer churning and chaotic. Instead, they had softened into a quiet, peaceful mist, drifting in calm waves across the horizon.

Nimbus smiled, his eyes warm with pride. "You did it, Charlie. You calmed the storm by facing each feeling and letting it go."

Charlie felt a lightness in his heart that hadn't been there before. "Thank you, Nimbus. I didn't realize how powerful my feelings were… or how much better I'd feel after letting them go."

Nimbus nodded. "Emotions are powerful, Charlie. They shape the world around us, just like they shape the clouds. When you take time to understand them, they become softer, easier to handle."

As they floated down to the ground, Charlie looked up at the gentle, grey clouds, feeling a deep sense of peace. He knew that he had learned something important about himself and about the sky—a way to find calm, even in the middle of a storm.

And as he lay back on the grass, watching the softened clouds drift by, Charlie knew that even on stormy days, he had the power to bring peace to his own sky.

Chapter 24: The Rainbow Cloud Festival

One bright morning, Charlie was in his backyard, gazing up at the sky when Nimbus drifted down with a look of pure excitement.

"Charlie!" Nimbus exclaimed, his misty form shimmering with colors. "Today is a very special day—the Rainbow Cloud Festival is about to begin, and you're the guest of honour!"

Charlie's eyes widened in delight. "The Rainbow Cloud Festival? What's that?"

Nimbus grinned. "It's a grand celebration held once every few years, when the clouds come together to create the most colorful, joyful display the sky has ever seen. It's a way for all the clouds to celebrate the beauty and magic they bring to the world. And because of everything you've done for us, you're our special guest this year!"

Charlie's heart filled with excitement. He couldn't believe he was about to be part of something so magical. "Thank you, Nimbus! I can't wait to see it."

Nimbus floated closer, his eyes twinkling. "Well, come along! There's so much to prepare, and everyone's excited to welcome you."

Charlie climbed onto Nimbus's misty form, and together they rose into the sky. As they climbed higher, Charlie began to notice clouds of every color gathering around them. There were clouds in shades of pink, blue, green, and yellow, all glowing with a soft, rainbow-like light. Each cloud shimmered with a vibrant hue, like they'd been painted with the colors of a sunset.

The air was filled with a joyful energy, and Charlie could hear soft laughter and cheerful voices as the clouds prepared for the festival. Colorful ribbons of mist and tiny sparkles floated in the air, giving the whole sky a feeling of celebration.

Nimbus guided Charlie to a grand, open area in the center of the clouds, where a soft, fluffy platform had been prepared just for him. "Welcome, Charlie, to the Rainbow Cloud Festival!" Nimbus announced proudly.

As Charlie took his place, the clouds gathered around, each one shining with its own unique color. A cloud shaped like a grand arch stretched above him, adorned with glistening droplets that sparkled like jewels.

The cloud nearest to him, a rosy pink one named Blossom, floated forward, her voice warm and welcoming. "Charlie, thank you for everything you've done for us. Because of your kindness, creativity, and bravery, the sky is brighter than ever. Today, we celebrate with you!"

The clouds all cheered, their voices soft and joyful, filling the air with a musical hum. Charlie felt his heart swell with happiness. "Thank you, everyone," he said, his voice filled with gratitude. "It's been an honour to explore the sky with you."

Blossom smiled and drifted back as Nimbus gestured to the gathered clouds. "Let the festivities begin!"

The first event was a grand cloud dance, where the colorful clouds began swirling and spinning, creating beautiful patterns in the air. Pink, blue, and golden clouds wove together, forming intricate designs that shimmered like a living rainbow. As they moved, tiny droplets of mist floated down, sparkling like confetti in the sunlight.

Charlie watched in awe as the clouds created shapes—a giant heart, a star, and a swirling spiral that seemed to reach all the way across the sky. The colors blended and shifted, forming new patterns with each movement. It was like watching a living painting, a display of beauty and magic that took his breath away.

Next, Nimbus floated over with a special surprise. "Charlie, it's your turn to join the festival! You'll get to create your own display with rainbow mists. Just hold out your hands and let your imagination guide you."

Charlie eagerly held out his hands, and a soft mist of rainbow colors began to form around them. He thought of all the wonderful things he'd seen in the sky, from the gentle sunset clouds to the vibrant Rainbow River. Slowly, he shaped the mist, creating a glowing rainbow arch that stretched high above him, filled with colors so bright they seemed to glow from within.

The clouds cheered as Charlie's rainbow lit up the sky, casting a warm, colorful light over the entire festival. Charlie laughed with joy, feeling the excitement of being part of something so magical.

After the rainbow display, the clouds gathered for a special tradition—the Rainbow Cloud Parade. Each cloud, dressed in its brightest colors, drifted through the sky in a grand procession, forming lines and shapes as they passed. Some clouds were small and delicate, while others were large and fluffy, each one carrying a unique shade of the rainbow.

As the clouds paraded past Charlie, they waved and sparkled, each one sending a burst of color in his direction. He waved back, his heart filled with gratitude and joy for all his cloud friends.

At the end of the parade, Nimbus floated over to Charlie, his eyes shining with pride. "Charlie, we have one final gift for you—a rainbow cloak made of mist, just for today. It will allow you to glow with the colors of the clouds, so you can truly be part of the festival."

Charlie's eyes sparkled with excitement as Nimbus draped the soft, rainbow mist over his shoulders. Instantly, he felt a warm, tingling sensation, and he looked down to see that he was glowing with every color of the rainbow, just like the clouds around him.

With his rainbow cloak, Charlie joined the clouds as they danced and spun in the sky, his colors blending with theirs in a joyful celebration. Together, they created a final, breathtaking display—an enormous rainbow that stretched across the entire horizon, filling the sky with vibrant hues that shimmered in the sunlight.

Below, people looked up, gasping in amazement as they watched the colorful spectacle. The entire town was filled with joy as they pointed at the sky, smiling at the beauty of the Rainbow Cloud Festival.

As the festival came to a close, the clouds gathered around Charlie, their voices soft and full of warmth. "Thank you, Charlie," they said, "for reminding us of the magic in the sky and for sharing your kindness with us."

Charlie felt a warmth in his heart as he looked at each of his cloud friends. "Thank you for inviting me," he replied, his voice filled with gratitude. "This has been the most magical day of my life."

Nimbus drifted over, his eyes shining with pride. "The Rainbow Cloud Festival is a celebration of all the colors, joy, and wonder in the sky. And today, you became part of that magic, Charlie. You'll always be one of us."

As Charlie floated back down to his backyard, his rainbow cloak fading softly around him, he looked up at the sky with a heart full of gratitude and joy. He knew that he would always carry the colors of the clouds with him, a reminder of the magic and friendship he had found above.

And as he lay back in the grass, watching the clouds drift by, Charlie knew that the sky would always be a place of beauty, wonder, and color, waiting to be celebrated by those who looked up.

Chapter 25: The Dream Clouds

One quiet evening, as twilight began to settle over the town, Charlie was lying on his favorite hill, watching the stars blink to life. The sky was a soft shade of deep blue, and the clouds floated gently, bathed in the silvery light of the moon. Just when he thought the night couldn't get more peaceful, a familiar misty form drifted down beside him.

"Nimbus!" Charlie said with a smile. "The sky looks so calm tonight."

Nimbus nodded, his eyes sparkling with a gentle glow. "Yes, Charlie. Tonight is special—it's the night of the Dream Clouds."

Charlie sat up, intrigued. "The Dream Clouds? What are those?"

Nimbus gave a soft, mysterious smile. "Dream Clouds are where dreams are born. Each night, the Dream Clouds carry tiny bits of magic from the stars and weave them into dreams. Those dreams drift down to children and fill their minds with wonder as they sleep."

Charlie's heart filled with excitement. "That sounds amazing! Can I see the Dream Clouds?"

Nimbus's misty form shimmered with delight. "Of course. Tonight, I'll take you to the place where dreams are made."

Charlie climbed onto Nimbus, and together they floated up into the night sky, higher than they had ever gone before. As they climbed, Charlie felt the air grow softer and quieter, as if they were entering a world made only of whispers and wishes.

Finally, they arrived in a part of the sky filled with shimmering clouds, each one glowing softly with a magical light. The clouds were different from any Charlie had seen before—they were faintly translucent, with shades of silver, lavender, and midnight blue swirling together like liquid starlight.

"These are the Dream Clouds," Nimbus whispered, his voice soft and reverent. "Each one holds a dream, ready to drift down to someone below."

Charlie looked around in awe, feeling as if he were standing in a magical realm. Tiny sparkles floated through the air, each one glimmering like a tiny star. As he watched, he saw that each sparkle held a faint image—a scene of a child running through a field, or a family laughing together, or an adventure in a far-off land. Each sparkle was a dream, just waiting to be shared.

"This is incredible," Charlie whispered, his eyes wide with wonder.

As he drifted through the Dream Clouds, Charlie noticed one small, shimmering dream floating nearby. It was a gentle, soft glow, with the faint image of a child flying through the sky, laughing with joy. The dream seemed a bit unsure of itself, flickering slightly as it drifted alone.

Charlie floated closer, his heart going out to the little dream. "Hello, little dream," he said kindly. "Are you lost?"

The dream sparkled faintly, as if it were shy. "I... I think I am," it murmured in a soft, gentle voice. "I'm supposed to find a child, but I don't know the way."

Nimbus floated over, watching the dream with a warm smile. "Some dreams need a little help finding their way. They carry a bit of magic, but they need a guide to reach their destination."

Charlie felt a surge of determination. "I can help! I'll guide you to the child you're meant for."

The little dream brightened, its glow growing a bit stronger. "Thank you, Charlie. I want to bring joy to someone... I just don't know how to get there."

Nimbus nodded in approval. "All you need is to follow your heart, Charlie. Think of the joy and comfort the dream will bring, and let that feeling guide you."

Charlie closed his eyes, holding the little dream gently in his hands. He pictured a child below, lying in bed, their eyes closed and waiting for the magic of a dream. He imagined the warmth and happiness the dream would bring, filling the child's mind with laughter and adventure.

As he focused, he felt a gentle pull, a soft tug in his heart that seemed to guide him downward. He opened his eyes, smiling at the little dream. "I know the way. Let's go!"

With Nimbus floating beside him, Charlie drifted down through the sky, the little dream glowing softly in his hands. As they descended, Charlie could feel the dream's excitement, its light growing brighter with each moment.

Finally, they reached a small house with a single window open to the night sky. Inside, a young child lay asleep, their face peaceful and calm, waiting for the magic of a dream.

"This is it," Charlie whispered, holding the dream gently. "Go on, little dream. It's time for you to bring joy."

The dream sparkled with gratitude, its soft voice full of warmth. "Thank you, Charlie. I'll remember this."

With a final shimmer, the dream floated gently out of Charlie's hands, drifting through the open window and settling over the sleeping child. As it touched the child's mind, the dream began to glow, filling the room with a soft, comforting light. Charlie could see the child smile in their sleep, their face filled with happiness as the dream took root, weaving a world of wonder in their imagination.

Charlie watched, feeling a deep sense of joy and fulfilment. He knew that the little dream would bring the child a night full of magic and adventure, filling their heart with warmth and happiness.

Nimbus placed a gentle hand on Charlie's shoulder. "You did something beautiful tonight, Charlie. You helped bring a bit of magic to the world below."

Charlie looked up at the Dream Clouds above, his heart filled with gratitude. "Thank you, Nimbus. I'll never forget this night."

As they floated back up to the Dream Clouds, Charlie looked around, seeing each cloud in a new light. He knew that every dream held its own magic, a tiny piece of wonder ready to bring joy and comfort to those who needed it.

When they returned to the Dream Clouds, the other dreams seemed to glow a little brighter, as if they, too, were grateful for Charlie's kindness. He felt a warmth in his heart, knowing that he had been part of something truly special.

As Charlie and Nimbus drifted back to his backyard, Charlie looked up at the night sky, his heart full of peace. He knew that the Dream Clouds would always be there, quietly weaving dreams for those below, bringing magic and joy to the world one dream at a time.

And as he lay back in the grass, watching the stars twinkle above, Charlie closed his eyes, filled with the memory of the Dream Clouds—a place where magic and wonder waited to be shared.

Chapter 26: The Cloud Library

One bright, breezy afternoon, Charlie was lying in the grass, watching fluffy white clouds drift lazily across the sky, when Nimbus appeared, looking particularly excited.

"Charlie," Nimbus began, his misty form shimmering with anticipation, "I have a special place to show you today—a place where the clouds keep stories."

Charlie sat up, his eyes lighting up with curiosity. "Stories? In the clouds?"

Nimbus nodded, his voice full of warmth. "Yes. It's called the Cloud Library. It's a library made entirely of clouds, where each wisp holds a story written in mist. Some clouds carry tales from long ago, while others capture moments from everyday life. The Cloud Library is a place where memories, dreams, and stories are kept for anyone who wishes to visit."

Charlie's heart swelled with excitement. "That sounds amazing! Can we go?"

Nimbus smiled. "Of course. Today, you'll have a chance to explore the stories of the sky."

With a grin, Charlie climbed onto Nimbus's misty form, and together they floated up into the sky. They drifted through soft clouds and gentle breezes, climbing higher and higher until they reached an area where the air seemed to shimmer with a faint, magical glow.

In front of them was a vast, wispy structure that looked like a palace made of mist. Towers and arches rose up from layers of soft cloud, and every surface shimmered with a faint silver light. Charlie could hardly believe his eyes—it was like a castle made of fog and stardust.

"Welcome to the Cloud Library," Nimbus said softly, gesturing to the grand structure before them.

As they entered, Charlie saw rows upon rows of misty shelves, each one lined with thin wisps of cloud, like rolls of soft parchment. Each wisp glowed faintly, its colors shifting and swirling as if it were alive with hidden stories.

Nimbus floated over to one of the shelves and gently lifted a small wisp from its place. "Every cloud wisp holds a story," he explained, handing it to Charlie. "When you hold it, the story will reveal itself, unfolding in your mind like a memory."

Charlie held the wisp carefully, feeling its cool, airy texture in his hands. He closed his eyes, and as he focused, a story began to appear in his mind—a tale of a young girl and her first snowy winter, filled with joy and wonder. He could see the girl's laughter, the sparkle of fresh snow, and the warmth of her family around her.

When he opened his eyes, the wisp glowed softly before fading back to a calm, silvery mist. Charlie let out a breath of amazement. "It's like I was there with her," he whispered.

Nimbus smiled. "That's the magic of the Cloud Library. These stories capture moments, memories, and dreams, preserving them in wisps so that they can be shared with others."

Charlie looked around, filled with excitement. "Can I read more?"

Nimbus chuckled. "Of course. Take your time and explore. Each wisp has a story waiting just for you."

Charlie wandered through the shelves, carefully picking up different cloud wisps. With each one, he discovered a new story—some were tales of grand adventures in far-off lands, while others were simple, quiet moments, like a family sharing a meal or a child discovering a new friend. Each story had its own magic, and Charlie felt as though he were traveling to different worlds with every wisp he held.

He came across one cloud wisp that glowed a soft, golden color. When he held it in his hands, he saw a memory of a young boy watching the sunrise for the first time, his eyes filled with awe as the sky changed from darkness to brilliant light. Charlie felt the warmth of the sun, the joy of discovery, and the peace of that quiet morning, as if it were his own memory.

As he continued exploring, he found wisps that carried ancient tales of the sky—the story of the first rainbow, the origin of the stars, and legends about the clouds themselves. One story told of a time when the sky had been dark and empty, until a single brave cloud spread color across the horizon, creating the first sunrise. Charlie could almost feel the pride and beauty of that moment as he held the wisp in his hands.

After a while, Nimbus drifted over, his eyes twinkling with kindness. "Charlie, would you like to add your own story to the Cloud Library?"

Charlie looked up, surprised. "I can add my own story?"

Nimbus nodded. "Yes. The Cloud Library is open to everyone who has something to share. You've had so many adventures with us, and your story would be a wonderful addition."

Charlie felt a rush of excitement mixed with a little nervousness. "How do I do it?"

Nimbus guided him to a special shelf made of soft, swirling mist. "All you need to do is think of the memory you want to share, then let it flow into the wisp."

Charlie took a deep breath, thinking of all the wonderful moments he'd shared with the clouds. He remembered his first meeting with Nimbus, the time he painted pictures in the sky, the adventure through the Rainbow River, and the night he helped a lost dream find its way to a child below. Each memory was filled with joy, wonder, and a deep sense of belonging.

As he held the empty cloud wisp in his hands, he let the memories fill him, one by one. Slowly, the wisp began to glow with a soft, colorful light, swirling with hints of pink, blue, and gold, like a miniature rainbow.

When he opened his eyes, the wisp was shining brightly, filled with the essence of his memories. Charlie placed it carefully on the shelf, his heart swelling with pride.

Nimbus placed a gentle hand on his shoulder. "Thank you, Charlie. Your story will be here for others to discover, a part of the sky's history."

Charlie looked at the wisp, feeling a sense of joy and fulfilment. "Thank you for bringing me here, Nimbus. This place is... magical."

Nimbus nodded, his voice soft. "The Cloud Library is a reminder that every life, every moment, is part of a bigger story. Each wisp holds a piece of the world, and together, they create a tapestry of memories and dreams."

As they floated back down to the earth, Charlie looked back at the Cloud Library, its misty shelves glowing softly in the distance. He knew that his story was now part of the sky, a gift he could share with others who visited that magical place.

And as he lay back in the grass, looking up at the stars, Charlie felt a deep sense of connection to the world around him. He knew that stories—whether big or small—had the power to bring people together, to inspire wonder, and to carry on through time.

In his heart, he felt a quiet joy, knowing that his adventures would always be part of the sky's endless story, a memory kept safe in the magical Cloud Library.

Chapter 27: The Invisible Cloud

One clear morning, Charlie was sitting outside, enjoying the warmth of the sun and the soft breeze that rustled through the trees. The sky was a bright, cloudless blue, and he was beginning to wonder if Nimbus might show up to share another adventure.

Just then, he felt a light, playful tickle on his cheek, as if a tiny wisp of mist had brushed against him. Startled, he looked up, expecting to see Nimbus or one of the other clouds, but the sky was still completely empty.

"Did you feel that, Charlie?" Nimbus's voice called softly as he floated down beside him, looking particularly thoughtful.

Charlie looked around, feeling the strange sensation again, like a faint, cool breeze swirling around him. "Yes, but... I don't see anything. Are you doing that, Nimbus?"

Nimbus shook his head, his misty form shimmering with a faint, knowing smile. "No, Charlie. What you're feeling is an invisible cloud—a cloud that's there, but only those who truly believe can sense it."

Charlie's eyes widened in surprise. "An invisible cloud? How can a cloud be invisible?"

Nimbus drifted closer, his voice soft and filled with mystery. "Some clouds are born with a special kind of magic. They exist just as other clouds do, but they remain hidden from view. To see an invisible cloud, you have to open your heart and imagination, trusting that it's there, even if your eyes can't see it."

Charlie's heart raced with excitement. He loved the idea of a cloud that was both there and not there—a hidden friend floating through the sky. "Can you help me see it, Nimbus?"

Nimbus nodded, his eyes sparkling. "Of course. Invisible clouds respond to belief, to the willingness to see beyond what's obvious. Close your eyes, Charlie, and take a deep breath. Imagine the shape of a cloud in your mind—something soft and gentle, like a breeze you can almost feel."

Charlie closed his eyes, letting go of his thoughts and focusing on the feeling of the air around him. He took a deep breath, picturing a soft, friendly cloud, light as mist, floating just in front of him. He imagined it swirling and shifting, as if it were waving at him, waiting for him to notice it.

Slowly, he began to feel a faint, cool touch against his skin, like the gentle brush of a breeze. It felt real, as if the invisible cloud were truly there, surrounding him with its soft, misty presence.

"Can you feel it, Charlie?" Nimbus asked softly.

Charlie nodded, keeping his eyes closed. "Yes... it feels so close, like it's right here."

"Now, open your eyes slowly," Nimbus instructed. "Look with your heart as well as your eyes."

Charlie opened his eyes, focusing on the space just in front of him. At first, he saw only empty air, but then, a faint shimmer appeared, like a wisp of mist catching the sunlight. As he concentrated, the shimmer grew stronger, and a shape began to take form—a soft, misty cloud, barely visible, but undeniably there.

Charlie gasped in awe. "I see it! It's... it's really there!"

The invisible cloud floated gently in front of him, swirling in delicate patterns, as if it were greeting him. It was faint and light, like a breath of air, but he could make out its soft edges, moving gracefully as it drifted beside him.

The cloud seemed to sense Charlie's excitement, and it gave a tiny, playful swirl, wrapping around him like a misty hug. He laughed, feeling a sense of wonder and joy at discovering something so magical, something hidden that only he could see.

Nimbus smiled, his eyes warm with pride. "You did it, Charlie. You opened your heart to see what others might overlook. Invisible clouds are special—they remind us that there's magic even in the things we can't see."

Charlie reached out, feeling the cool touch of the invisible cloud against his fingers. "Hello, friend," he whispered, feeling a bond with the gentle, hidden cloud. "You're beautiful."

The cloud seemed to shimmer in response, swirling around him in a playful dance. Charlie laughed, reaching out as it brushed gently past him, creating a feeling of lightness, as if he were floating along with it.

Nimbus floated beside him, his voice soft and kind. "Invisible clouds are shy, but they're also full of kindness. They often bring comfort to those who are feeling alone, even if people don't realize they're there."

Charlie nodded, understanding the cloud's quiet, comforting presence. "Thank you for showing yourself to me," he said softly, feeling a deep sense of gratitude. "I'll never forget you."

The invisible cloud shimmered once more, swirling around him in a gentle goodbye before drifting slowly upward, blending seamlessly with the sky. Though he could no longer see it, Charlie could still feel its presence, like a soft memory lingering in his heart.

Nimbus placed a gentle hand on Charlie's shoulder. "Remember, Charlie, that not everything important can be seen. Sometimes, the things we feel are just as real, even if they're invisible."

Charlie looked up at the sky, feeling a quiet joy in his heart. He knew that, even though he couldn't see the invisible cloud anymore, it would always be there, a hidden friend watching over him from above.

And as he lay back in the grass, gazing up at the vast, blue sky, Charlie knew that the world was filled with hidden wonders, waiting to be discovered by those who were willing to believe.

Chapter 28: A Cloudy Birthday Surprise

It was a bright, sunny morning, and Charlie was just finishing his breakfast when he noticed something unusual in the sky. The clouds seemed to be gathering in a way he hadn't seen before, forming clusters and shapes that looked like they were planning something big.

Curious, Charlie stepped outside, feeling the warmth of the sun on his face. Just as he was wondering what was going on, a familiar misty form drifted down from above.

"Happy Birthday, Charlie!" Nimbus exclaimed, his eyes twinkling with excitement.

Charlie's eyes widened in surprise. "Nimbus! You remembered my birthday?"

Nimbus chuckled, swirling in a playful circle. "Of course we did! Today, the clouds have a very special surprise planned just for you."

Charlie's heart filled with joy as he looked up at the sky, watching as more clouds gathered, each one shimmering with hints of color and light. "A surprise? What is it?"

Nimbus winked. "If I told you, it wouldn't be a surprise! Come along and see for yourself."

With a grin, Charlie climbed onto Nimbus, and together they floated up into the sky. As they rose higher, he saw clouds of all shapes and sizes gathering in one grand, open area, each one glowing with excitement. There were fluffy cumulus clouds, wispy cirrus clouds, and even a few tiny, misty clouds that sparkled with little droplets of water.

Blossom, the pink-tinted cloud he had met before, drifted over with a warm smile. "Happy Birthday, Charlie! We've all come together to make this a special day for you."

Charlie beamed with happiness. "Thank you, Blossom! This is already the best birthday I've ever had."

Nimbus gestured to the clouds around them. "Today, we're throwing you a Cloudy Birthday Party! We've prepared a few surprises, starting with a very special sky display."

Charlie watched with eager eyes as the clouds began to take their places, each one moving gracefully across the sky as they prepared for the show. Slowly, the clouds arranged themselves in the shape of a giant heart, each one glowing softly with hints of pink and blue.

A gentle hum filled the air as the clouds began to move, swirling and shifting in perfect harmony. The heart shape grew larger, and then it transformed into a giant star, sparkling with tiny droplets that caught the sunlight, creating a dazzling display that shimmered across the entire sky.

Charlie gasped in delight, feeling his heart swell with joy. "It's beautiful!" he exclaimed, watching the clouds change from one shape to another, each one more magical than the last.

Next, a group of rainbow clouds floated in, releasing a soft mist that spread across the display, filling the sky with vibrant colors. The colors blended and swirled, creating a rainbow that arched gracefully across the horizon, like a ribbon of light dancing through the sky.

As the rainbow faded, the clouds gathered together once more, forming the shape of a giant birthday cake, complete with misty "candles" that glowed softly with golden light. The entire sky looked like a celebration, filled with color and light that seemed to pulse with joy.

Charlie laughed with delight, clapping his hands as he watched the display. "Thank you, everyone! This is the most amazing birthday surprise!"

Blossom drifted over, carrying a small, fluffy gift wrapped in a soft, misty bow. "And here's a little something from all of us, Charlie—a cloud crystal."

Charlie took the gift, marveling at the delicate crystal nestled in the cloud. It sparkled faintly, like a tiny piece of the sky captured in his hand. "Thank you, Blossom! It's beautiful."

Nimbus smiled warmly. "The cloud crystal is a symbol of friendship. As long as you have it, you'll always carry a piece of the clouds with you, no matter where you are."

Charlie held the crystal close, feeling a warmth in his heart. "I'll treasure it forever. Thank you, all of you."

To end the celebration, Nimbus floated to the front, his voice clear and joyful. "Now, let's finish with a Cloud Dance!"

The clouds began to swirl and spin, moving together in graceful arcs as they performed a dance across the sky. They formed shapes and patterns, creating waves and spirals that filled the air with a joyful rhythm. The sky was alive with movement and color, a celebration that felt as magical as it looked.

Charlie joined in, spinning and laughing as he floated among his cloud friends. Together, they danced across the sky, each movement filled with happiness and joy. He felt like he was part of something wonderful, a celebration not only of his birthday but of all the beautiful moments he had shared with the clouds.

As the dance came to a close, the clouds gathered around Charlie, their voices soft and full of warmth. "Happy Birthday, Charlie!" they cheered, filling the sky with a chorus of joy.

Charlie looked around, his heart full of gratitude. "Thank you, everyone. This has been the best birthday I could ever imagine."

Nimbus drifted over, placing a gentle hand on Charlie's shoulder. "You're part of our sky family, Charlie. Today, we wanted to remind you of how special you are to us."

Charlie smiled, feeling a deep sense of belonging. He knew that the clouds had become more than just friends—they were a part of his life, a magical world that he would always carry in his heart.

As he floated back down to his backyard, the sky was filled with soft colors and gentle light, a final gift from his cloud friends. He looked up, waving goodbye as they drifted back into the horizon, their forms glowing softly in the fading light.

And as he lay back in the grass, holding his cloud crystal close, Charlie knew that this birthday would be a memory he would cherish forever—a day when the clouds came together to celebrate with him, filling the sky with magic, joy, and love.

Chapter 29: The Cloud Creator's Workshop

One sunny afternoon, Charlie was lying in the grass, watching the clouds drift lazily across the sky. He was daydreaming about all the different types of clouds he'd seen—fluffy cumulus, wispy cirrus, even the rainbow-colored clouds from the festival. Just as he was imagining what it would be like to create a cloud of his own, he heard a familiar, gentle voice.

"Charlie!" Nimbus called as he floated down, his eyes twinkling with excitement.

Charlie sat up, smiling. "Hi, Nimbus! I was just thinking about how amazing all the clouds are. It would be fun to design one myself someday."

Nimbus's face lit up. "Well, today might just be your lucky day. How would you like to visit the Cloud Creator's Workshop?"

Charlie's jaw dropped in excitement. "The Cloud Creator's Workshop? There's a place where clouds are made?"

Nimbus chuckled, swirling in a playful circle. "Yes! The Cloud Creator's Workshop is a magical place where new clouds are dreamed up, shaped, and brought to life. Each cloud starts as a simple wisp and is carefully crafted into a unique shape, color, and texture. Today, you'll get the chance to design your very own cloud."

Charlie's heart raced with excitement. "Really? I'd love that!"

Nimbus gave him a misty hand to climb onto, and together they floated up into the sky. As they travelled, Charlie noticed a new part of the sky he'd never seen before—a soft, glowing area filled with silvery light. In the center of this magical space was a grand, misty building that looked like a giant workshop made entirely of clouds.

"Welcome to the Cloud Creator's Workshop," Nimbus announced, gesturing to the airy structure in front of them.

Charlie's eyes widened with wonder as they entered. The workshop was filled with tables made of soft, fluffy clouds, each one covered in wispy tools and glowing materials. There were jars of rainbow mist, trays of sparkling droplets, and even tiny paintbrushes made from the finest mist. Around the room, other cloud creators were busy at work, shaping, swirling, and crafting beautiful clouds of all sizes.

One of the creators, a gentle, silvery cloud named Zephyr, floated over with a warm smile. "Hello, Charlie! Nimbus told us you'd be visiting today. Are you ready to create your very own cloud?"

Charlie nodded eagerly. "Yes! I've never made a cloud before, but I can't wait to try."

Zephyr led him to a large, fluffy workbench and handed him a small wisp of mist, no bigger than a cotton ball. "Every cloud starts as a simple wisp," Zephyr explained. "With a little imagination and care, you can shape it into anything you'd like. Just let your creativity guide you."

Charlie held the wisp in his hands, feeling its soft, cool texture. It was light and delicate, almost like holding a tiny piece of air. He thought about all the different clouds he'd seen and wondered what kind of cloud he wanted to create.

After a moment of thought, he began to shape the wisp, using his fingers to gently mold it. He decided to make a cloud that was a little bit of everything—a fluffy, playful shape with soft, rounded edges like a cumulus cloud, but with wispy trails like cirrus clouds that floated in the wind.

Zephyr watched him with an approving smile. "Wonderful, Charlie! Now, let's add some color. Here in the workshop, we have rainbow mist that can give your cloud any shade you can imagine."

Zephyr handed Charlie a small jar filled with shimmering rainbow mist. Charlie opened it, dipping his fingers in and letting the colorful droplets spread across his cloud. As he worked, he added touches of soft pink and golden yellow, with hints of lavender along the edges. The colors blended together beautifully, creating a cloud that looked like a piece of the sunset sky.

As he added the final touches, Charlie noticed a small tray of glittering droplets labelled "Special Effects." Curious, he turned to Zephyr. "What's this for?"

Zephyr smiled. "Those droplets add a touch of magic. You can choose from a soft glow, a hint of sparkle, or even a gentle, misty shimmer. Just sprinkle a little onto your cloud, and watch it come to life."

Charlie carefully picked up a few droplets of shimmer and sprinkled them over his cloud. Instantly, the cloud began to glow softly, its colors shining with a warm, gentle light. It looked magical, like a cloud you might see in a dream.

Nimbus floated over, his eyes wide with admiration. "Charlie, it's beautiful! You've created a cloud that's unique and full of personality."

Charlie beamed with pride, feeling a deep sense of accomplishment. "Thank you, Nimbus. I wanted it to be something special."

Zephyr nodded approvingly. "Your cloud is ready, Charlie. Now, let's take it outside and let it float in the sky."

Together, they carried the cloud out of the workshop and into the open sky. Charlie released it gently, watching as it drifted upward, glowing softly as it took its place among the other clouds.

The cloud floated gracefully, its colors shimmering in the sunlight as it moved through the air. Charlie felt a rush of joy, knowing that he had created something beautiful that would become part of the sky.

Nimbus placed a gentle hand on his shoulder. "Every cloud in the sky tells a story, Charlie. Yours will add a bit of wonder and color to the world, reminding others to look up and dream."

Charlie watched as his cloud drifted higher, blending into the horizon, a piece of his creativity and imagination now part of the vast, endless sky.

As they floated back down to the earth, Charlie felt a deep sense of peace and fulfilment. He knew that his cloud would always be up there, a special creation that he could look for whenever he gazed at the sky.

And as he lay back on the grass, watching the clouds drift by, Charlie knew that the world was full of endless possibilities, each one waiting to be shaped by those who dared to dream.

Chapter 30: The Day the Sky Turned Pink

One afternoon, as Charlie was lying in his backyard looking up at the bright blue sky, he noticed something unusual. A faint pink mist was spreading across the horizon, growing brighter and more vibrant with each passing moment. The color was unlike any sunset he'd ever seen—it was a playful, rosy pink, filling the sky with a soft, magical glow.

Charlie sat up, his eyes wide with surprise. "What's going on?"

Just then, Nimbus appeared, his misty form swirling with excitement. "Hello, Charlie! It looks like someone's made a bit of a mess in the sky today," he chuckled, his eyes twinkling with amusement.

Charlie looked up at the rosy clouds above. "A mess? You mean this pink sky wasn't supposed to happen?"

Nimbus nodded, glancing around with a knowing smile. "That's right. One of the younger clouds, Puff, got a little too excited in the Cloud Creator's Workshop and accidentally spilled an entire jar of pink mist!"

Charlie laughed, watching as the pink mist spread even further. "So that's why the whole sky looks like cotton candy!"

Nimbus grinned. "Exactly! Puff thought he'd be able to make a small pink cloud, but as soon as the jar tipped over, the mist spread everywhere. Now the entire sky has turned a lovely shade of pink."

Charlie couldn't help but smile at the sight. "I think it's beautiful. The pink color makes everything look warm and happy."

Just then, a small, fluffy cloud floated over, looking sheepish as he drifted around in small circles. Charlie guessed that this must be Puff—the cloud responsible for the pink sky. Puff was a round, puffy little cloud, and even though he looked embarrassed, he couldn't seem to hide a hint of pride at the accidental beauty he'd created.

"Puff, this is Charlie," Nimbus said, introducing them. "Charlie, meet Puff, our playful pink cloud artist."

Charlie smiled, waving up at the little cloud. "Hi, Puff! I love what you've done with the sky. It's like a dream up there."

Puff swirled in a shy circle, his soft voice filled with a mix of pride and nervousness. "I... I didn't mean to spill all the pink mist. I just wanted to make a tiny pink cloud, but then... well, now the whole sky is pink."

Nimbus patted Puff's fluffy form reassuringly. "Accidents happen, Puff. Sometimes, the best surprises come from unexpected things. The sky is more colorful today, and it's bringing joy to everyone below."

Charlie looked around, noticing that people in his town were pointing up at the sky, their faces filled with smiles and wonder. He saw children laughing and pointing, neighbours stepping outside to take photos, and even a few birds soaring happily through the pink-tinged air.

"See, Puff?" Charlie said, pointing to the happy faces below. "Everyone loves it! Sometimes, a little bit of playfulness can make the world feel brighter."

Puff perked up, swirling in a happy spiral. "Really? So... the pink sky isn't a problem?"

Nimbus chuckled. "Not at all, Puff. In fact, why don't we make the most of it? Today can be 'The Day the Sky Turned Pink'—a celebration of unexpected beauty!"

Charlie's eyes sparkled with excitement. "Can we add some more colors? Maybe make it look like a pastel rainbow?"

Nimbus nodded, floating up beside Puff. "Let's do it! Charlie, you can help us guide the colors across the sky."

Together, Charlie, Nimbus, and Puff set to work, carefully adding soft, pastel colors to different parts of the sky. They started with a gentle lavender mist, blending it with the pink to create a gradient that stretched from one end of the horizon to the other. Then, they added hints of soft peach and pale yellow, letting the colors melt into each other like the strokes of a giant painting.

Puff grew more confident as he worked, swirling the mist with a joyful energy. He spun around, creating delicate trails of color that filled the sky with soft, glowing patterns.

Charlie and Nimbus guided the colors, shaping them into gentle waves and spirals that seemed to dance across the sky. The result was a breathtaking display—a pastel masterpiece that filled the entire sky, creating a scene that looked like it had come straight from a dream.

People below watched in awe, their faces filled with joy and wonder as the pastel colors swirled and shimmered above. Some children began to twirl and dance, pretending to reach up and touch the colors, while others lay back on the grass, gazing up in amazement.

Charlie felt a warmth in his heart as he looked around, knowing that they had created something special. "This is amazing, Nimbus. It's like a whole new kind of sky."

Nimbus nodded, his eyes shining with pride. "Today is a reminder that sometimes, accidents can lead to beautiful surprises. Puff's playfulness created a sky that no one will forget."

Puff gave a happy swirl, his voice filled with pride. "Thank you, Charlie and Nimbus. I thought I'd made a mistake, but now I see that a little fun can make the sky even more magical."

As the sun began to set, the pastel colors grew softer, blending with the evening light. The entire sky glowed with a gentle, rosy hue, a final gift from Puff's playful accident.

Charlie looked at the sky, feeling a deep sense of peace and joy. "Thank you, Puff. This was a perfect day."

Nimbus floated over to Charlie, placing a gentle hand on his shoulder. "And thank you, Charlie, for helping us make this day even more special. The pink sky will always be a reminder that beauty can come from the most unexpected moments."

As they floated back down to the ground, Charlie took one last look at the pink sky, watching as it faded into the soft colors of twilight. He knew that he would always remember this day—the day the sky turned pink, filling the world with warmth, playfulness, and the joy of an unexpected adventure.

And as he lay back in the grass, watching the stars begin to twinkle, Charlie knew that the world was full of surprises, each one waiting to be discovered and celebrated.

Chapter 31: Goodbye to Nimbus

It was a crisp morning, and Charlie was out on his favorite hill, watching the clouds drift lazily across the sky. He noticed Nimbus approaching, his form moving a bit slower than usual, almost as if he were carrying a weight in his misty heart.

"Nimbus!" Charlie called out, waving. "Is everything alright?"

Nimbus drifted down, a gentle smile on his face, but Charlie could sense something different in his eyes—a softness, a hint of sadness. Nimbus hovered close, looking at Charlie with a mixture of pride and tenderness.

"Charlie," Nimbus began, his voice soft and kind. "There's something I need to tell you. Soon, I'll be traveling to another part of the world."

Charlie felt his heart drop. "You're... leaving?"

Nimbus nodded, his misty form shimmering faintly. "Yes. As a cloud, it's my duty to bring rain, shade, and a bit of wonder to different places. It's time for me to move on and bring my magic to new skies. There are towns and fields that need rain, children who need a friend, and skies that need color."

Charlie tried to hold back the sadness welling up inside him. Nimbus had become his dearest friend, a constant presence of joy and magic in his life. The thought of the sky without Nimbus felt empty and strange.

"But... I'll miss you," Charlie whispered, his voice barely audible. "The sky won't be the same without you."

Nimbus drifted closer, resting a gentle, misty hand on Charlie's shoulder. "And I'll miss you, too, Charlie. You've been a wonderful friend, and I'll always carry the memories of our adventures in my heart."

Charlie felt a tear slip down his cheek. "We've had so many good times, Nimbus. I don't know if I can look at the sky without thinking of you."

Nimbus gave him a warm, reassuring smile. "Remember, Charlie, that even though I may not be here, you'll always carry a part of me in your heart. The sky is full of friends, clouds, and stories. And every time you see a cloud drift by, think of it as a reminder that I'm still out there, bringing joy and wonder to someone else."

Charlie took a deep breath, feeling a mixture of pride and sadness. He understood that Nimbus had a purpose beyond their friendship—a duty to spread his magic to other parts of the world. And as much as it hurt, he knew he had to let Nimbus go.

"Will I ever see you again?" Charlie asked, his voice filled with hope.

Nimbus's eyes sparkled softly. "The world is a big, beautiful place, Charlie, but clouds travel far and wide. Who knows? Perhaps one day, I'll drift back over this hill, and we'll meet again. Until then, remember all we've shared, and know that our friendship lives on in every cloud you see."

Charlie nodded, trying to hold back the tears, but feeling his heart grow heavy. "Thank you, Nimbus, for everything. You've shown me magic, beauty, and wonder. I'll never forget you."

Nimbus's misty form glowed softly, as if he, too, was holding back his own feelings. "Thank you, Charlie. You've been a friend like no other, and our adventures have filled my days with joy."

They stood there for a few moments, neither one wanting to say the final goodbye. Charlie took one last look at his friend, memorizing the gentle swirl of his mist, the shimmer of kindness in his eyes, and the warmth that radiated from his presence.

Then, with a final, soft smile, Nimbus began to drift up, his form growing fainter as he rose into the sky. "Goodbye, Charlie," he called, his voice carrying like a soft breeze. "Keep looking up. I'll always be just a cloud away."

Charlie watched as Nimbus floated higher and higher, his misty form blending with the morning sky. He felt both sadness and gratitude, knowing he had been part of something truly special—a friendship that had changed his life.

As Nimbus disappeared into the horizon, Charlie whispered one last goodbye, feeling the warmth of their memories filling his heart. He knew that every time he looked up at the sky, he would see Nimbus in the clouds, a reminder that friendship, like the sky itself, was boundless and ever-present.

And as he lay back in the grass, watching the clouds drift by, Charlie promised himself that he would carry Nimbus's spirit with him always, a piece of magic he could cherish, no matter where the wind took his friend.

Chapter 32: A New Cloud Friend

It had been a few days since Nimbus had left, and Charlie was feeling the quiet emptiness of his absence. He missed the familiar sound of Nimbus's voice, the gentle swirl of mist that had always filled the sky with warmth and magic. Every time he looked up, he found himself hoping to see Nimbus drift by, but the sky was empty of his friend.

One afternoon, as he lay on the grassy hill, looking up at the passing clouds, Charlie sighed. "I wonder where you are now, Nimbus," he whispered, feeling a pang of loneliness. The sky had lost a bit of its sparkle without Nimbus by his side.

Just then, he noticed a small, puffy cloud drifting toward him. This cloud was different from the others—round and soft, with a faint, silvery glow and a playful shape that seemed to bounce in the air. It moved toward him with a cheerful energy, as if it had something to say.

Curious, Charlie sat up and waved. "Hello there! Are you new around here?"

The cloud gave a little spin, as if in greeting, and floated closer, hovering just above Charlie's head. It was a small cloud, with fluffy edges and a soft, silvery mist that sparkled faintly in the sunlight. Charlie couldn't help but smile at its bright, joyful presence.

"My name's Charlie," he said, reaching out a hand as if to shake with the little cloud. "Do you have a name?"

The cloud swirled happily, giving off a soft hum, and a faint voice drifted to his ears. "I'm Cirra," the cloud whispered in a sweet, airy voice. "I was just passing by, and I couldn't help but notice you looked a little lonely."

Charlie felt his heart lift, surprised and delighted by the friendly cloud's kindness. "I was feeling a bit lonely," he admitted. "I had a friend named Nimbus, but he had to travel to another part of the world."

Cirra bobbed up and down, her misty form glowing with a gentle warmth. "I know Nimbus! He told me all about you, Charlie. He said

CHARLIE AND THE COLOURFUL CLOUDS

you were one of the kindest friends he'd ever met and that the sky was brighter because of you."

Charlie felt his face light up with joy. "Nimbus talked about me? That makes me feel... a little less lonely."

Cirra swirled closer, wrapping a gentle, misty tendril around his hand. "Nimbus knew you'd miss him, so he sent me to keep you company. I may not be as big and wise as Nimbus, but I'd love to be your friend."

Charlie's heart filled with gratitude. "Thank you, Cirra. I'd love to be your friend, too. You have such a happy, bright spirit—you remind me of a silver star."

Cirra twinkled, her mist shimmering like stardust. "I love that! Maybe I can be a 'star cloud' for you, bringing a little light whenever you need it."

Charlie laughed, feeling the warmth of a new friendship filling the space Nimbus had left behind. "That sounds perfect."

The two spent the rest of the afternoon playing together, with Cirra drifting and twirling around him, shaping herself into playful patterns and silly faces that made Charlie laugh. She could make herself look like a giant, smiling moon, or a silly cat with big, round eyes. Each time she changed shape, she'd give a little sparkle, as if she were winking at him.

"Wow, Cirra, you're so good at transforming!" Charlie said, clapping his hands with delight as Cirra formed a little rainbow above his head.

Cirra giggled, swirling with joy. "Thank you! My favorite thing is to bring a bit of sparkle to those who need it."

As the sun began to set, casting soft pinks and oranges across the sky, Cirra floated beside Charlie, watching the colors with him. "You know, Charlie," she said softly, "Nimbus may be far away, but you'll always have friends in the sky. Each cloud carries a piece of the world with them, and that includes the love and memories we share."

Charlie nodded, feeling a warmth in his heart. "Thank you, Cirra. I didn't think anyone could replace Nimbus, but you're not here to replace him, are you? You're here to remind me that the sky has room for new friends, too."

Cirra gave a soft, happy hum. "Exactly! Friendship isn't about filling an empty space—it's about making new memories and keeping the old ones close."

Charlie looked up at her, his heart filled with a deep sense of peace. "I think I understand now. Friends come and go, but each one brings something special. And each one leaves a little bit of magic in my heart."

As the last rays of sunlight faded into dusk, Charlie lay back in the grass, watching the stars begin to twinkle. Cirra floated beside him, her silvery mist blending with the soft light of the evening sky. He knew that, no matter where Nimbus was, he'd always be part of his life—and now, he had Cirra to share new adventures with.

Charlie smiled, closing his eyes as he felt a gentle, misty touch brush against his hand. He knew that the sky was filled with friends, both old and new, each one adding their own special magic to his world.

And as he drifted off to sleep, he dreamed of clouds and stars, of friends near and far, and of a sky that was boundless and full of love.

Chapter 33: Back to the Sky

It had been some time since Charlie had last seen Nimbus or even his new friend, Cirra. He'd enjoyed many wonderful adventures with the clouds, each one leaving a special place in his heart. But lately, he hadn't been able to float up into the sky quite as often, and he found himself missing his cloud friends more than ever.

One evening, as he lay on his favorite hill watching the stars appear, Charlie sighed. The sky was vast and beautiful, but it felt so far away. He wondered if he'd ever be able to visit the colorful clouds again.

As if sensing his thoughts, a gentle, familiar voice drifted down. "Charlie..."

Charlie sat up, his heart lifting with hope. "Nimbus?"

And there he was—Nimbus, swirling gently in the evening sky, his misty form glowing softly under the light of the stars.

"Nimbus!" Charlie exclaimed, jumping to his feet. "I missed you!"

Nimbus floated down, resting a soft, misty hand on Charlie's shoulder. "I missed you too, Charlie. The sky has been bright with memories of you. And though I may travel far, you'll always be welcome here."

Charlie's eyes filled with wonder. "But I haven't been able to visit as often. I thought maybe I couldn't come back..."

Nimbus gave him a warm, reassuring smile. "Charlie, the sky is always here for you. All you need to do is keep dreaming, keep believing, and you'll be able to visit us whenever you wish. The door to the sky is in your heart."

Charlie's heart swelled with happiness and relief. "You mean... I can come back anytime? Even if I'm just lying here on the hill?"

Nimbus nodded, his eyes sparkling. "Yes, Charlie. The clouds remember you, and every time you close your eyes and imagine, every time you look up with wonder, you're with us. The magic of the sky lives in your dreams."

Charlie took a deep breath, feeling a warmth settle over him. He closed his eyes, letting his imagination drift up into the sky. He pictured himself floating beside Nimbus, watching the soft pinks and golds of the clouds, hearing the laughter of Cirra, and feeling the gentle warmth of the sun.

And then, he felt it—a gentle breeze, a soft touch, and the cool mist of the clouds around him. He opened his eyes and found himself surrounded by familiar faces. There was Nimbus, Cirra, and even Blossom, the rosy pink cloud, all smiling at him, each one glowing with joy.

"Welcome back, Charlie!" Cirra chimed, twirling playfully in the air.

Blossom drifted close, her pink mist swirling warmly around him. "It's so good to see you again, Charlie. The sky has missed your light."

Charlie felt tears of joy prickling his eyes. "Thank you, everyone. I didn't know I could visit you like this, just by dreaming."

Nimbus floated beside him, resting a comforting hand on his shoulder. "Dreams are powerful, Charlie. They can take you anywhere you want to go. And as long as you keep dreaming, the sky will always be here for you."

The clouds gathered around, creating a colorful display just for him. They drifted in patterns and shapes, forming a heart, a star, and a soft wave that washed gently across the sky. They shimmered with colors, glowing softly under the light of the moon.

Charlie watched in awe, his heart filled with happiness. He knew that even though he couldn't be with them every day, he could visit whenever he needed to—whenever he felt a longing for the magic and friendship of the sky.

As the evening grew deeper, the clouds began to sing a soft, comforting lullaby, their voices blending like a gentle breeze. Charlie lay back, letting the sound wash over him, a melody that seemed to wrap around his heart like a warm hug.

And as he closed his eyes, he knew that no matter where he was, the sky would always be there, just a dream away. The clouds, his friends, would be waiting, ready to welcome him back with open arms.

As he drifted off to sleep, Charlie whispered, "Goodnight, Nimbus. Goodnight, Cirra. I'll see you in my dreams."

And as the stars twinkled above, the clouds floated high in the sky, carrying the joy of Charlie's visit with them. They knew that he would always be with them, in spirit and in dreams, their friendship as boundless and timeless as the sky itself.

Disclaimer:

This book is a work of fiction created for entertainment and educational purposes. All characters, events, and settings are products of the author's imagination and are intended to spark creativity, curiosity, and joy in young readers.

Any resemblance to real persons, living or deceased, or actual events is purely coincidental. While the story features imaginative adventures with clouds, please remind children that climbing on clouds or trying to interact with them in real life is not possible. This book encourages children to dream, imagine, and explore within the safe and magical world of storytelling.